Oh Father, you've got to save me!

Oh Lord, Noah's soul cried in anguish.

"Jailer!" he called, desperate for relief from the inky darkness. "My candle has gone out. Please, bring another."

The silence persisted.

"Jailer!" the prisoner shouted again and shook the door of his cell until it clattered like a collection of tin cans in a feed sack.

The creak of a swivel chair and feet hitting the floor preceded a grumble and the turn of a key in the office door. As the door opened, a shaft of weak light penetrated the darkness. "Wha-da-ya-want?" the jailer inquired, his voice slurred with sleep. He squinted toward Noah, his thinning, gray hair rumpled from the long night.

"My candle is out."

"Go to sleep then." The old man rubbed his face, shadowed from need of a shave.

"Could you sleep, Lester, if you were waiting to be hung?" The words left Noah nauseous, and he wondered if his mother would ever learn what had happened to him.

DEBRA WHITE SMITH lives in East Texas with her husband and two small children. She is an author and speaker who pens both books and magazine articles and has twenty-five book sales to her credit, both fiction and nonfiction including *More than Rubies* (Beacon Hill Press) and *The Seven Sister Series* (Harvest House). Debra holds a B.A. and M.A. in English and has hundreds of thousands of books in print. Both she and her novels have been voted favorites by **Heartsong Presents** readers. *Texas Angel* is the final series book to *Texas Honor, Texas Rose,* and *Texas Lady.* A portion of her earnings from her writing goes to Christian Blind Mission, International. You may visit Debra on the World Wide Web at www.debrawhitesmith.com.

Books by Debra White Smith

HEARTSONG PRESENTS
HP237—The Neighbor
HP284—Texas Honor
HP343—Texas Rose
HP356—Texas Lady

Heartsong Presents Readers' Service
PO Box 719
Uhrichsville, OH 44683

Texas
Angel

*Debra White Smith
with Robert Osborne*

Heartsong Presents

For my own little angels—Brett and Brooke.

A note from the author:
I love to hear from my readers! You may correspond with me by writing: **Debra White Smith**
Author Relations
PO Box 719
Uhrichsville, OH 44683

ISBN 1-57748-958-6

TEXAS ANGEL

All Scripture has been taken from the King James Version of the Bible.

Cover illustration by Jocelyne Bouchard.

PRINTED IN THE U.S.A.

prologue

(Taken from *Texas Lady*, Heartsong Presents #356)

Dogwood, Texas. June 1886

Magnolia faintly tapped on Rachel's closed bedroom door. "Hello, Rachel?" she called gently. "It's me, Maggie. May I come in?"

A familiar face appeared on the other side of the door. "Rachel's asleep right now," Angela Isaacs whispered, "but do come in." Her chestnut-colored hair and freckled nose testified to Angela's and Rachel's kinship. But that's where the cousins' similarities ended. While Rachel was fiery, Angela had always been more reclining. Angela, slender and tall, carried herself gracefully, but seemed to dwarf the petite Rachel when the two stood side by side.

Magnolia stepped into the room to see the lace curtains waving in front of the numerous bedroom windows. The large wicker fan lying on the foot of Rachel's bed attested to Angela's having fanned her cousin while she slept.

"How is she doing, Angela?" Maggie asked.

"Well, she cried herself to sleep." Angela paused to blink back the tears. "But I believe the elixir Dr. Engle left this morning has helped her sleep in peace for the first time since the labor started last night. She's been asleep a couple of hours now."

"Bless her," Maggie said, astounded at how drawn Rachel's pale face appeared. And the bright sunshine spilling through the windows only highlighted the dark circles marring her eyes. Once again, Maggie was reminded that she didn't hold the exclusive rights to trouble. About a year ago, Rachel's father had died, leaving her alone to tend to this expansive land. Now, she and Travis had lost their first child—a little girl, according to Dr. Engle.

"Is there to be a funeral?" Magnolia asked.

"No. Travis and Dr. Engle buried the baby this morning, out in the pasture, under one of the trees."

"And Rachel? Did she see the baby?"

Angela nodded, her eyes filling with tears.

The patient stirred, and Magnolia stepped to her side to notice dots of perspiration along Rachel's forehead. "Are there some damp cloths for her face? She looks terribly hot."

"Yes," Angela said, moving to the door. "Travis just brought in a fresh bucket of cold well water not long ago. I'll go get some of it and bring some cloths as well."

"Magnolia?" Rachel breathed, stirring restlessly.

"Yes, I'm here." Maggie knelt beside the feather bed and encircled Rachel's hand within her own.

At last, Rachel opened her eyes to look up at Maggie with doe-like agony. "It w–was a little—little girl," she said, tears dampening her cheeks.

Remembering her own mother's pain-filled inscriptions about the deaths of her twin sons, Maggie nodded. Somehow, being with Rachel at this moment gave Maggie a sense of connection with the mother she had never known.

"Dr. Engle has—has been like a—a father to me." Rachel's voice cracked as she wrinkled her brows.

"I think he's like a father to most of Dogwood, Rachel," Maggie said. "He's a wonderful, wonderful man."

"Yes. . .but I—I can tell when—when he's withholdin' bad news. I'm afraid there's somethin' t–terribly wrong. That—that perhaps I won't ever be able—able to have children. It's just this h–horrible feelin' I have that I can't—I can't get over."

Wondering what she should say, Maggie grappled with an appropriate reply. As usual, the stirrings of inadequacy plagued her. *What do I say? How much should I tell her? Exactly how certain is Dr. Engle that Rachel mustn't try to bear children?* At last, Maggie decided that now was certainly not the time to share more disheartening news with the devastated Rachel.

"I'm not as—as experienced with these types of things as Dr. Engle, but—but he wouldn't have left you this morning if he didn't think you were going to be fine. He'll be back out to check on you before dark this evening. You can tell him your concerns then. I'm sure he'll be glad to answer all your questions. Right now, you just need to focus on recoverin'." Maggie gripped

Rachel's hand all the tighter and hoped she did not push for more information concerning the dim prognosis.

Spiritlessly, Rachel stared out one of the open windows. "I know I sh–shouldn't doubt the—the Lord, Maggie," she said, her voice gaining strength the more she talked. "But I think I must be the worst doubter in the world. Sometimes I just don't understand why He allows all the sufferin' and—and death. I didn't think I'd ever get over Pa's death. Now—now this!" She turned imploring eyes to Maggie. "Doesn't the Lord think we would make good parents? Is there something I've done wrong? I want a baby more than anything. And if—if just supposin' I can't—I'll feel as if I've let Travis down in the worst of ways."

"Yes, I understand, but. . .I'm sure the Lord will somehow. . ." Maggie didn't know what to say. So fresh were her own questions about God and life that she could do nothing but hold Rachel's hand and silently support this childhood friend. "I'll certainly keep you in my prayers," Maggie encouraged. "If—if you'll remember me as well."

Rachel nodded in understanding. "We can be a support to one—one another." Her head tilted to the side. Her heavy eyes closed. And her breathing became steadier.

Praying for Rachel's strength and her own wisdom, Magnolia thoughtfully observed her friend, slipping into the folds of sleep. And with the cattle's soft lowing flowing through the opened windows, an idea, like a tiny cloud, presented itself on the horizon of her mind.

At a breathtaking pace, that cloud gained size. . .size and definite plausibility.

Louella Simpson was due to give birth very soon. She had no idea what she was going to do once the baby arrived. She had no means of supporting the child. She even said that returning to her hometown would heap ridicule upon her mother and herself. So, she couldn't go back home. But just suppose. . .just suppose Louella loved her child so much she would be willing to place it in Rachel's loving arms? Precious few people in Dogwood knew about Louella. Only key people had privy to the fact that Rachel had even miscarried. Rachel and Travis could very easily accept Louella's baby as their own, and the child would never bear the shame of the label, "illegitimate." No one in Dogwood needed ever to know the child was adopted.

The sound of Angela entering the room disrupted Maggie's thoughts, but in no means dismissed the exciting possibilities. . .if only Louella would agree.

"I'm sorry it took so long," Angela said in her usually tranquil tones. "But Travis and his brother. . .um. . ." She squinted as if she were searching for his name.

"Levi," Maggie supplied while Angela poured the cool water into the stoneware washing bowl on the bedside table.

"Yes, Levi." Angela's brown eyes glittered with the romantic speculations that Magnolia had seen all over town. Was no one in Dogwood left without knowledge of Magnolia's personal life? "The two of them were inquiring concerning Rachel," the schoolteacher said.

Her words, as precise as always, reflected her studious nature and the academic excellence to which she pushed her students.

"I'm so hot," Rachel muttered, stirring from her light sleep.

Maggie dipped one of the clean, although stained, cloths into the well's icy water and gently patted Rachel's forehead.

"Thank you," Rachel mumbled. Taking the cloth from Maggie, she stroked her neck and cheeks as well. "It's so p–powerfully hot today." She produced a languid smile, which hinted at her usually playful nature. "I heard you. . .talking about Levi," she said, her voice once more gaining strength with each word she spoke. "Angela, Levi is c–courting Maggie. Did you know?"

Shocked, Magnolia glanced from Rachel to the speculative Angela, and back to Rachel.

"We–we're going to be sisters-in-law, I think," Rachel continued.

"Yes, that's what I hear," Angela said in a scheming voice. "Yesterday at the quilting bee—"

"We aren't courting," Maggie blurted, recalling Levi's brief embrace, which suggested the opposite.

"Then may–maybe he'll court Angela." Rachel's feeble wink left Maggie glad to see some of the redhead's spunk, although her chagrin increased all the more.

"Even from her sick bed, she torments me," Angela said. "I'm an old maid, and I will remain that way all my years. I'll probably go to my death before trusting a man again."

"Ah, Angela, one d–day somebody as good as my Trav's gonna come along and. . .and make you forget you ever said that." Rachel raised her head and Maggie automatically placed another pillow behind her. Perhaps the patient would even feel like sipping some broth for her noon meal.

Glancing toward the blanching Angela, Maggie recalled the tragic story beneath the sudden stoniness in her eyes. She had been jilted ten years before, when Maggie was just past adolescence. Now thirty, the mildly attractive schoolteacher stood little chance at matrimony, and spinsterhood apparently suited her.

one

Rusk, Texas. September, 1888

The faint ticking of the worn clock hanging on Sheriff Garner's office wall wormed into Noah Thorndyke's brain until his head throbbed with an incessant ache. Suddenly the clock's hammer tolled ten doleful times. *One for each hour I have to live,* Noah thought. *Oh God, help me!* he despaired, his soul feeling as if it would rend in twain.

The jail cell smelled of sweaty, straw-filled mattresses. Mildew clung to the walls like the sooty cloak a hangman wears. A lone window on the opposite side of the cell admitted a few lonely night sounds: crickets, a dog barking at some menace, and owls hooting in the East Texas woods. Noah, condemned to die, sat on the edge of a cast iron bunk and gazed in despair at the wrinkled wanted poster that bore his exact likeness. However, the name beneath the image was Rupert Denham, not Noah Thorndyke. Meager light from a candle, sputtering in protest over the inferior tallow, cast a pale glow of dappled light across the poster. As Noah had wondered a thousand times, so he wondered now, *Who is Rupert Denham and why does he look so much like me?*

Noah's eyes burned with a combination of fury and foreboding, and the tension in his gut testified to his soul's despair. He and this Rupert Denham shared the same square jaw line. The same dark hair and eyes. The same straight nose and prominent brows—like that of a Greek sculpture. The only difference between Noah and this Rupert was the scraggly mustache that made his counterpart appear villainous. Noah always kept himself cleanly shaven.

He ran long, artistic fingers through his neck-length hair then slapped his knee, crumpled the poster, and stood. As he had all day, Noah wondered how his call to preach had culminated in such a tragic and unfair ending. *Sentenced to hang. . .I have been sentenced to hang.* The facts seemed less the product of reality and more the results of a tortuous nightmare.

Room for only two steps in either direction made pacing difficult. But confinement tortured him, so persistent movement provided some measure of relief. Nagging thoughts of the next few hours crumbled in a useless heap. The candle's flame dwindled. Ghostly shadows lost their outlines and mingled with the uneven texture of the rock walls.

Fatigue bore into his every muscle, producing a nervousness impossible to calm. He stopped walking and with sweaty palms gripped the bars on the cell door. The cold bars, smooth from the wear of callused skin on iron, seemed a metaphor for the chill in Noah's spirit. Many others must have experienced the despair of lonely hours waiting for rough hemp to squeeze the last breath from their throats. The candle popped a final time then lost its battle with the darkness—a darkness that settled around Noah, seeping into his soul like the kiss of death itself.

Oh Lord, Noah's soul cried in anguish. *Oh Father, you've got to save me!*

"Jailer!" he called, desperate for relief from the inky darkness. "My candle has gone out. Please, bring another."

The silence persisted.

"Jailer!" the prisoner shouted again and shook the door of his cell until it clattered like a collection of tin cans in a feed sack.

The creak of a swivel chair and feet hitting the floor preceded a grumble and the turn of a key in the office door. As the door opened, a shaft of weak light penetrated the darkness. "Wha-da-ya-want?" the jailer inquired, his voice slurred with sleep. He squinted toward Noah, his thinning, gray hair rumpled from the long night.

"My candle is out."

"Go to sleep then." The old man rubbed his face, shadowed from need of a shave.

"Could you sleep, Lester, if you were waiting to be hung?" The words left Noah nauseous, and he wondered if his mother would ever learn what had happened to him.

"You're gettin' what you deserve. Shootin' our banker!" Lester eyed Noah with a condescending glare. "No better man ever lived than William Frank. They can't hang you quick enough for me!"

"Like I told the judge, I didn't have anything to do with that murder," Noah argued, a fresh surge of frustration rushing upon him as he recalled that horrid trial. Never, had Noah been so aghast at how lies could sound so truthful.

"I've heard that plenty of times from men standin' right where you are, and it don't make no difference. I'll get your candle," he ground out. "But it's just 'cause I'm tired of yer bellowin'. Otherwise, I'd say get used to the dark. The place you're goin' is blacker than night, or so I've been told."

"Would you get me a deck of cards too?" Noah asked, hating to resort to the deceptive plan that was slowly inching its way into his thoughts. But at this point, Noah felt he had no choice. He could wait for an unjust death or use artifice to gain his freedom.

"What?" Lester's bushy brows rose. "You been tellin' everybody you're a preacher man. How do ya square that with card playin'?"

"Just a little solitaire to keep my mind off. . .you know." Noah shrugged.

"Humph. Figures." Lester growled. "There's some cards in the sheriff's desk. Anything to keep you quiet so I can get some shut-eye." He yawned and rubbed his balding head. "I'll be back in a minute."

Lester clicked the door closed then turned his key in the lock with the squeaking sound of metal against metal. The noise reassured Noah that Lester carried his keys with him at all times. His plan for escape might work, and work well. He busied himself thinking through each step until the rusty lock once more protested against Lester's key.

Holding the flickering candle, the jailer passed Noah the cards. He walked toward the window across the room, removed the spent candle from its tin holder, and dropped the stub on the floor. In seconds, he forced the fresh, burning candle into the holder and turned to face Noah, the glow of the lone flame behind him.

"Do I get any food?" Noah asked. "I didn't get dinner or supper, and breakfast was lean as well, for that matter." His stomach growled as if to punctuate his plight. No one in these parts seemed too concerned about the livelihood of a prisoner whom they were certain was a murderer.

"Not 'til morning. And, don't expect much then. Where you're goin' you won't need much to eat!" the jailer barked, walking toward the door.

Smiling, Noah spoke as kindly as he dared. "Say old-timer, do you like card tricks?" He expertly shuffled the deck and put the cards through a battery of fancy moves.

"Devil's work! And if you was any kinda preacher, you wouldn't be so familiar with that deck." Lester hitched up his droopy britches with one hand and suspiciously eyed Noah. "Where'd ya learn to do all that, anyway?"

"I spent a lot of time on the river when I was a kid." Noah continued the shuffling, all the while hating the feel of the cards in his hands. Years had past since he had shuffled a deck. Years. . .but the skill came back to him as if he had played poker only yesterday.

"I know'd you weren't no preacher!" Lester sneered.

"A man can change. That's what the Bible teaches." The cards pattered together in a patterned cadence and Noah shuffled them again.

"Didn't work for you," the jailer grumped and started for the door.

"Watch the ace of spades disappear." Noah's toes curled inside his boots. If this plan worked, he would be free in a matter of minutes. Free, to prove his innocence.

The old man looked back, a hint of curiosity in his faded, gray eyes. Noah fanned the deck with only the ace of spades staring at the jailer. He closed the fan very slowly. When he reopened the deck the ace had disappeared.

"Gimme them cards!" The old man stepped forward and carefully inspected each one. Noah expertly inserted the ace into the man's pocket. "Where's that ace?"

"Look in your shirt pocket," Noah said smugly.

Lester reached toward his pocket, his double chin bunching under his neck. He fumbled in the folds of his shirt and pulled out the ace of spades. "Glory be! How'd you do that?"

"My secret," Noah said with a grin. "Now, here's another trick, but you've got to come close."

Mesmerized by Noah's slight-of-hand, the simple jailer pressed into the bars, his gaze fixed on the cards. In one deft move Noah reached through the rungs and slipped the jailer's pistol from its holster. Dropping the deck, he gripped the jailer's belt. Yanking him up to the bars, Noah spoke softly but firmly. "Ease over to the door and you'll unlock it, right?" His heart pounding, Noah wondered what he would do if the old man refused. He certainly would never use the gun.

Lester's baggy eyes bulged like a frog's. His lips trembled. His breath came out in short, wheezing bursts. "Of—of course," he stuttered and shuffled toward the door. He slipped the key in the lock and turned the shaft. With a metallic grunt the bolt moved and the bars swung out.

Noah released his grip. "Get in here," he commanded, loathing the taste of every word. Stepping aside, Noah allowed Lester to move into the cell. "Take off your shirt and tear two strips from the bottom."

The old man, whimpering like pup, began the tedious task. The sound of tearing fabric reflected the ache in Noah's soul. He detested having to play the scoundrel. Noah Thorndyke was a man of God, not some ruffian. *Oh Lord, forgive me,* he prayed. *Forgive me if I am doing wrong, but I don't want to hang. You know as well as I do that I'm not a murderer.*

As the old man tore the final strip from his shirt, Noah recalled his musings as he prepared for the journey from Louisiana to Tyler, Texas, mere weeks ago. He had prayed that, perhaps, this trip would introduce him to the woman whom God intended him to marry. Noah was so tired of his lonely existence. He hungered for the completeness only a godly wife would bring to his life. Ironically, instead of a woman of God, Noah had encountered a sentence of death.

The jailer finished his task and helplessly stared at his prisoner.

"Stuff one strip in your mouth," Noah ordered. "Tie the other around your head to hold the gag in." He waited while the jailer complied. "Now we're going to the office nice and quiet." Waving the gun barrel toward the door, Noah allowed the jailer to precede him.

Once through the door, Noah spotted a pair of handcuffs, blotchy with rust, hanging from a spike in the wall. "Get those cuffs," he growled then waited as Lester, his shoulders slumped in defeat, obeyed the command. If only the old man could detect just how severely Noah was shaking and how reticent he was even to place his finger against the trigger, he would have never complied. Noah prayed like a madman that he could continue this facade until he secured his freedom.

"Now, walk back toward the cell, nice and slow," Noah said.

As if he could read Noah's mind, Lester cast a speculative glance toward his captor.

"Now!" Noah snarled.

The old man jumped and grunted then shuffled toward the door.

Within minutes, Noah fettered Lester's hands behind his back and locked the jail cell. He paused before making his exit and spotted a worn Bible lying on the thin mattress. "I'm sorry to do this to you old fellow. I really am. And if it makes you feel any better, I wasn't lying when I said I am a man of God. I'd have never shot you, and I want you to know how much I appreciate your cooperation."

Lester, glaring at Noah, produced a long string of grunts that sounded strongly like cursing.

"The Lord can sure help you with your feelings over all this," Noah said through a perverse, wobbly chuckle. "And I'll point you to that Bible the sheriff lent me. It will guide you down the right paths." He nodded toward the leather-bound book, lying on the mattress. "Meanwhile, I'll put your pistol on the sheriff's desk. Don't want to run off with anything that doesn't belong to me. You'll find your keys with the pistol."

Noah retreated, stepped through the office doorway, and closed the door behind him. As the weight of what he had done settled around his shoulders, Noah's heart thudded like the steady pounding of wild horses, galloping upon a path, well trodden. Even during his years of adolescent rebellion, Noah had never broken the law to this degree. "But it was break the law or have my neck broken by the hangman's rope," he muttered, despising the choice he had been forced to make.

He stepped toward the cluttered desk and deposited the pistol and keys on it. Trying to run from the guilt that plagued his spirit, Noah rushed toward the front door, eased it open, and peered onto the street. Behind him, the Seth Thomas produced a broken chime, announcing that ten thirty had arrived.

Noah scanned the shadowed road, deserted except for a group of horses, three hundred yards away, tethered outside the saloon. Clanking piano music, raucous laughter, and faint, feminine squeals floated from the saloon. His hands producing a thick film of sweat, Noah stepped onto the boardwalk. He needed only to gain entrance into the horse livery up the lane, reclaim the steed that was rightfully his, and make his escape. *Lord, please extend Your grace but a few minutes more,* he prayed as he raised his collar, hunched his shoulders, and began the brief journey toward the livery, toward his freedom.

two

Dogwood, Texas

Angela Isaacs winced as she tugged her brush through long waves of tangled hair, the color of chestnuts. Despite the relentless snags, her persistence won, resulting in a gleaming cascade of silky tresses reaching her waist. She gazed at her own reflection in the mirror and noted the few crows' feet that were forming around her eyes. The lamplight, flickering from her bedside table, accented her best feature—the deep, auburn hair, so like her mother's.

She recalled many nights brushing her mother's long, flowing curls. During these hours away from the prying ears of her older brothers, Angela asked many womanly questions and begged for the tales her mother recounted with fiery passion. Some stories reflected memories from childhood. Others were fairy tales. Then, there were the Bible stories, which especially lit her mom's face with the glow of faith and love. But that was long ago. The demanding duties of Angela's teaching, coupled with the disappointments of the past, left her spending less and less time with God. Certainly, Angela attended church. That was part of the fulfillment of her contract as a schoolteacher. But for

Angela, an intimate relationship with the Lord now settled as a pale memory on a distant horizon.

The early September breeze now dancing through the opened window promised cooler days to come. Angela stepped toward her bed's fluffy feather mattress, lowered the lamp's wick, and settled against the down pillow. With the sound of crickets shrieking near her window, Angela watched the shadows dancing on the ceiling. Shadows that seemed a specter of her past.

Visions of her childhood blended with vague forms projected by the dim light. There were happy faces: her father, playfully tugging at her mother's apron strings and kissing her neck, just below her ever-present bun; her brothers, begging their dad to forego the day's work and take them hunting for rabbits and squirrels; a mother's careful needlework which produced the lovely dresses few other girls of Angela's station could afford. The images spoke of security and warmth. Warmth and love. Love and promise.

But the promise of childhood had faded in the light of the grown-up reality. A dark, leering figure from twelve years ago broke into her memories. Angela, desperate to block out the image of her former fiancé, closed her eyes, and coaxed herself to relax. As in the past, she buried her pain in the deepest recesses of her soul until she eventually found escape in the arms of slumber.

But this night, as with many others, the recollections of her deepest heartache—a heartache that left Angela determined to never again trust a man—were vividly reenacted in her dreams. . .

. . .Jason Wiley rode into Dogwood with saddle-bags full of law books and a story of an eastern education. He attended church every Sunday and finally picked Angela as the girl he liked best. She never uttered a prayer without thanking God for this wonderful man. There were picnics and square dances and hints of marriage. Sitting by Jason during the church elicited dreams of a home and children.

But on the Tuesday before Christmas, Angela's six months of bliss turned to ashes. She drove the family buggy into town that afternoon and purchased some last minute items for the special meal her mother always made on Christmas Eve. Jason had bought a new suit and would sit across the table so his eyes could melt her heart again. She knew for certain that he planned to speak with her father that night. Along with Angela, the whole town had fallen for Jason with his dark hair and sparkling blue eyes. Consequently, his law practice grew each day. Jason's success would encourage Papa to bequeath his consent for his daughter's matrimony.

Although knowing she might interrupt a client, Angela *had* to drop by his office that Tuesday. She decided that if she could not steal one of his warm, tender kisses, she would discreetly blow him one from her fingertips. The bell jingled merrily as she stepped through the door and into the small, outer office. An uneasy silence settled about the quarters like the faint gasp of an insulted matron. Muffled noises, oozing with the nuance of impropriety, drifted from Jason's main office. A rolling chair, gliding across the hard wood floor, accompanied a suppressed giggle.

"Jason?" Angela called. "Are you there?"

"Just a minute," he shouted.

The caution in his voice left Angela's stomach churning with misgivings. "Is everything all right?"

A second giggle brought a tingle to the back of Angela's neck and left her legs weak. Jason's oak office door stood open by only inches. As if propelled by some unseen force, Angela stepped around the small secretary's desk and approached the door. Her fingers shaking, she pushed against it. Complaining with a coarse creak, the door swung inward to reveal a faded couch in the room's shadowy corner. Leah Marsh, the barmaid at the saloon, sat in a disheveled heap. A silly smile adorned her painted face. Jason stood by the window trying to get his shirt buttoned. Traces of lip rouge left their telltale prints around his mouth, cheeks, and even on the right earlobe.

"Angela. I—I can. . .explain," he stammered.

"Explain!" Angela gasped, feeling as if her soul had been ripped out and trampled by a thousand stampeding stallions. "Explain!" she erupted again, choking back a disillusioned sob. "This scene does–

doesn't need any—any explanation. You won't *ever* ex–explain anything to me—me *again*." She stumbled back, grasped the knob, and slammed the door shut. The sound made a thud in her heart like a steel curtain dropping on the stage of her life.

The few feet to the front door felt like a day's journey through a dense, briar-filled forest, infested with vipers and carnivorous beasts. Angela trudged past the thorns of depression, the pits of heartache, the crags of worthlessness, before finally gripping the knob that would lead her to the boardwalk, to her waiting horse and buggy. Confusion, dense as a cold fog, descended upon her as she clambered onto the driver's bench.

Forgetting other errands, Angela wheeled the buggy around and headed for home. Once out of town, the sobs tore at her soul, seeming to shred her spirit with every eruption. The road turned into a watery blur while the gray mare strained forward in abeyance to her furious urging. As they neared her parents' homestead amidst flying dust and a creaking buggy, Angela, at last, slowed the exhausted animal. The buggy rolled to a shuttering halt, and Angela plunged into the house, racing directly to her room. Her bitter crying lasted well into the night.

The day after Christmas, Angela's father called on Jason's office. The next day, her three brothers paid a visit of their own. By the first of the year, Wiley left town and no one ever saw him again.

Although everyone was kind, weeks of personal anguish and months of public humiliation dogged Angela. In spite of her parents' spiritual support and her questioning prayers, the bitterness of betrayal severely hindered her healing process. God had seemingly given Angela the man of her dreams, only to allow him to be yanked away. Jason Wiley had played a cruel trick on her. Her scarred heart never beat as softly again.

Mother and Father sacrificed to make a new life possible for Angela. Three days after her twentieth birthday they sent her to Houston College for Teachers. Her wounds closed, but never completely healed. The delights of watching her pupils learn slowly became the focus of her life. The happy faces of her current students paraded across the field of her dreams, each busy at spelling, reading, or math. . .

. . .The pain of her past bubbled to the surface again and tore her spirit with new rivers of tears. "No. . .no. . . no. . . Why, Jason, why. . ." she muttered, shifting from side to side until she gradually gained consciousness. Her hair, damp with tears, clung to the sides of her face, and the sheet and quilt tangled around her legs as if she had been running in place. Angela, sitting up, gazed around the simple room, rubbed her eyes, and wondered when these horrible nightmares would cease. During the past years, they had reduced themselves to only two or three times a year, but Angela was tired of even that much. Frustrated, she dashed aside the disheveled covers and stood.

The light of the full autumn moon sent rays of golden honey flooding into Angela's room through an open window. She padded across the floor and stilled the fluttering curtains long enough to pull the window shut against the cool, September breeze. Rubbing her arms, Angela walked toward her dresser and picked up the watch she wore on a chain around her neck. Squinting, she tilted the watch toward her window and saw the eleven o'clock hour swiftly approaching. She could not have been asleep more than half an hour.

With a faint groan, Angela deposited the watch back on the tatted doily and walked to her bed. In defeat, she lay on the feather mattress, sinking deeply into its folds as she sank into an equally deep despair. During the light of day, Angela could convince herself that she was completely over Jason Wiley. Even now, she conjured images of him in her mind and was pleased with the lack of romantic notions his form evoked. Perhaps Angela's problems lay less with leftover love for Jason, and more with leftover agony from the wounds he inflicted.

Her adolescent dreams of true love now seemed nothing but a mockery. At age thirty-two, those fantasies had dimmed to infrequent moments of hope, followed by fearful doubts. Occasionally, brief longings for the love of an honest man did flood Angela's heart, but the visions usually wandered down the misty road of "never mind." She looked toward the vacant spot beside her and wondered if she really wanted to grow old alone. Then, the anguish rose from the pits of her soul once more. *Alone. . .yes, alone is better than risking more heartache.*

The thought of agreeing to marry a man left Angela drowning in panic. Her younger cousin, Rachel Campbell, had recently told Angela that the Lord could help remove the haunting shadows from her eyes. But Angela was not sure she *wanted* them removed. She had hidden behind those haunting shadows and thus kept her heart safe for many years. So Angela clung to the shadows. They would continue to shield her for decades to come.

With a defeated sigh, she placed her hands behind her head. Tomorrow was Friday, filled with reports, testing, and lessons. But before school, she needed to check the pumpkins, sweet potatoes, and other vegetables in her fall garden. Alone. . .Angela would check the garden alone.

આ

In Rusk, Noah hurried down the shadowed boardwalk and paused at the corner before crossing a pathway, which led to an alley between the buildings. After five easy strides, he mounted the next wooden walkway and continued his hurried mission toward the livery, toward his horse. At last, the livery stable came into sight. Noah, his mind whirling with prayers and panic, sprinted from the boardwalk and neared the structure that appeared to be a small, red barn with closed double doors.

Surreptitiously, he glanced over his shoulder before testing the door. It swung inward with a faint sigh, exposing Noah to the smells of horseflesh and hay. His pulse pounding in anticipation, Noah entered the structure and strode straight toward the row of stables lining the back wall. He had placed his horse here two days ago and told the owner he would only spend one night in Rusk. Then, the first morning in town, he had been nabbed for murder.

Frantically, Noah peered into each stable, desperate for any sign of his coal black gelding. His boots shuffled against the hay-strewn floor and seemed to produce enough sound to awaken the whole town. *Oh Lord,* he prayed while finding a dappled gray in the next to the last stable, *tell me that man didn't sell my horse when he found out I was supposed to hang.* Only one stable remained, and Noah pondered his limited options should that stable not hold his steed. He could either steal one of the horses or see how far he could get on foot. As Noah approached the final stable, he decided he really did not have a choice. Noah could not steal a horse. Breaking from jail had been bad enough—but he was innocent. Noah would not turn to horse thievery. Holding his breath, he peered into the stable to see the great, dark eyes of his ebony mount gazing back at him. Midnight whinnied, and knocked an anxious greeting with one hoof against the stall's floor.

Noah suppressed a shout of victory. "Hello, boy. Miss me?" he whispered instead, extending his hand to stroke the horse between his eyes. The horse huffed out his nose and raised his head, his ears pricked. Noah turned the wooden latch and the door swung outward.

"Listen," Noah said under his breath. "I need you to run like you've never run in your life. Understand, ol' boy? We don't have a second to spare."

Noah retrieved his saddle, which hung on the wooden rail, and silently slipped it on the horse's back. Midnight pranced restlessly as if he were anticipating his mission. At last, with the saddle fastened and Midnight's bit in place, Noah led the horse across the spacious livery, toward the slightly ajar front door.

"We've almost made it," he soothed, his mouth as dry as Texas dust. "Almost. . ." He opened the door, led Midnight into the shadows, and mounted his steed. As he swung the animal around, he could almost taste victory. Then, a voice from within the livery bellowed, "Horse thief!"

His victory turning to despair, Noah rammed the heels of his boots into the gelding's sides. In response, Midnight bolted up the street.

"Horse thief! Horse thief! Help!" the man roared, and a hound joined in with a course of offended barks.

"Come on, come on, boy, run!" Noah urged, jamming his boots even deeper into the horse's side. His ears back, the horse surged forward, ever faster.

But the steed was not fast enough. Before Midnight galloped thirty yards, the loud report of a pistol attested to the livery owner's fury. A searing pain tore at Noah's side, and he gripped the saddle horn to keep his balance. "Oh dear Lord, I've been shot," he ground out. "Save me!"

Another bullet whizzed past his head, and a turn in

the road could not have come at a better moment. Noah, leaning forward, clung to the saddle horn with one hand, and clasped the reigns in the other. The horse continued its northward journey, and every breath racked Noah's body with a jagged blade of pain. A warm ribbon of blood inched its way across his waist and down his thigh as a growing fog seeped into his brain.

Time blurred as Noah pushed Midnight to the end of his endurance. The longer they traveled, the more Noah leaned upon the horse. At last, his cheek pressed into the gelding's damp hair, and the animal's exhausted wheezing seemed an echo of Noah's own labored breathing. After several miles of galloping, the horse reduced his rate to a canter. When the hours of morning approached, Midnight slowed to a walk. Eventually, his steps grew shorter, until he stopped and seemed to quietly estimate which of them would move next.

Struggling to think, Noah rubbed his gritty eyes and peered at his surroundings. The eastern horizon, pale from the approaching sun, produced faint illumination, but not enough to penetrate the shadows. All Noah's foggy mind could acknowledge was that somewhere in their journey, they had wandered off the road and into what might be someone's garden.

Midnight shifted his weight as if he were weary to the bone. "I'm sorry, boy," Noah muttered, his tongue thick. "So, so sorry." The blackness in his mind pushed back the feeble light of concentration. The combination of pain and loss of blood, along with lack of food and water took their toll upon Noah. He loosened his hold on the saddle, slowly collapsing onto a bed of cool, damp vines. Inky darkness wrapped its heavy cloak around his troubled spirit.

three

Shortly after dawn, Angela stepped out her back door and fitted the calico bonnet on her head. In seconds, she fashioned the ties into a snug bow under her chin and looked toward her fall garden. A heavy, autumn due covered the piney, east Texas hills and attested to the cool night temperatures which bore the kiss of autumn. By noon, Angela fully expected the hint of summer heat. But for now, she would enjoy the cool air.

She retrieved the small, sharp hoe from near her back door and walked toward the fall garden, full of pumpkins, tomatoes, turnips, and sweet potatoes. In the distance, a whippoorwill serenaded the rising sun that created a rainbow of colors on the eastern horizon. At the garden's edge, Angela paused to savor the morning smells clinging to her work dress: the scent of earth, the freshness of her garden, the aroma of coffee.

Angela's expectant cat, Grey, produced a faint meow and rubbed against her ankles. "Hello, kitty," Angela said, bending to scoop the animal into her arms. Grey purred and rubbed her face against Angela's. The cat had been a great companion for Angela during the last few weeks. She had arrived on the teacher's steps in August and Angela eventually realized the cat would soon produce a few more "friends."

"Did you come to help me work?" Angela asked, depositing the feline at her feet. With a disinterested air, the cat trotted toward the house as if to incite Angela to provide her usual saucer of milk.

Smiling, Angela gripped the hoe and stepped into the garden, ready to tackle the weeds that had arrived in the last few days. A classic folk song she planned to teach her students poured from her rich, alto voice. The tune danced among the brittle shafts of corn, left over from summer, and echoed against the deep orange bowls of ripening pumpkins. Angela gently hoed out the weeds and examined the growing autumn vegetables for signs that they were ready to harvest.

The fall tomatoes, toward the center of the garden, pled for her attention. The obnoxious grasses, vying for nutrition, seemed to have sprung up overnight. Angela viciously applied the hoe to the weeds, while noting with satisfaction that she would have ripened tomatoes within the week. She continued her song, digressing to a merry yodel from time to time.

Her hoe, striking against a reddish rock, produced a heavy clank, but another noise, like a swishing in the dried cornstalks, diverted Angela's attention. Pausing, she straightened and strained to listen, but heard only the faint, swishing breeze. She turned back to her task and took two more steps before the rustling in the corn stalks stopped her again. Angela's demanding schedule had prevented her from removing the stalks from the corner of her garden after the corn had stopped producing.

Now, something was awkwardly moving through the weed-infested stalks. That something was, most likely, a raccoon.

With the hoe poised, Angela cautiously edged toward the quivering stalks. She had never killed a coon. They reminded her too much of cats, and she loved cats. But Angela certainly held no qualms about scaring the daylights out of any coon. She stopped within inches of the corn and weeds, raised her hoe and yelled, "Get out of here, you nasty varmint!" Angela drove the hoe against the ground to produce a pounding threat, sufficient to scare the most daring of coons. The hoe hacked aside a layer of weeds to reveal the face of a man—not a coon.

"P–please," the man faintly begged. "I've—I've b–been shot. H–Help me." The man's face contorted into a painful grimace.

"What are you doing here?" Angela gasped, her mind whirling with shock.

"They—they w–were going to—to hang me in—in Rusk. I–I'm innocent," he said, panting with every word. "C–couldn't—couldn't let them h–hang me." He swallowed hard. His dark brows knitted together. He squinted as if concentrating were a monumental task.

Angela weakly leaned on her hoe and suspiciously scanned the countryside. The hair on the back of her neck prickled as she pondered the possibilities. This whole situation might be a trap of some sort. Her gaze settled once more on the man, whose face had fallen against his arm. *But what if he's telling the truth?* Angela wondered what it would feel like to be falsely accused of murder: the panic, the horror, the terror.

"W–water. . .I need—need water," the man rasped, reaching toward her laced work boot. "P–please. . . p–please help—help me." He gazed upward, his dark eyes full of pain. Pain and questions. Questions and desperation.

Impulsively, Angela knelt beside him and pushed away the intruding weeds, only to discover that they were smeared with blood along his right side. "You *have* been shot," she muttered, examining the tattered shirt, stained red.

"Y–yes."

With shaking fingers, Angela gently pulled away the shredded shirt to see what appeared to be a deep flesh wound, still oozing with blood. She winced as the man moaned. "I'm—I'm sorry."

"I–I need. . ." He trailed off, and a final look into his agonized eyes prompted Angela to make a decision. The strong lines of his square jaw, shaded with whiskers, suggested a man of honor who, at the moment, required assistance. She would aid him. Then, she would most likely notify the authorities. If he were indeed innocent, he should somehow prove that to the sheriff. Meanwhile, Angela's compassionate nature left her no choice. The same woman who took in an expectant, stray cat. . . the same woman who sat up late sewing dresses and shirts for students in need. . .the same woman whose heart would not allow her to kill a coon. . .that same woman would help this ailing stranger.

"I'm not sure I know what to do with you," Angela

said, as if she were talking with herself. "I've never treated a gunshot wound before. Maybe Dr. Engle—"

"No." His firm refusal came with more spunk than he had yet expressed. "If—if you can j–just give me—give me food—food and w–water and—and a b–bandage. . . and a night's—night's rest. . .I'll—I'll be on my—on my way."

The liquid brown eyes now beseeching Angela seemed full of anything but murderous intent—only gentleness and goodness, touched with distress. The vertical lines between his heavy brows spoke of a man of thought, a man of quiet but intense power. The curve of his lips suggested a sensitive spirit. Something in his voice urged her to give him a chance. . .to trust his word.

But her rooster's raucous crow from near the schoolhouse seemed a metaphor for Angela's recurring past. Once she *had* trusted a man. Trusted with all her heart. That trust had resulted in her betrayal, heartache, devastation. *You are crazy to even consider helping this man!* a rational voice urged. *He probably is a murderer. Leave him here! Wait until the school children arrive, and have one of them go for Constable Parker.*

"J–just one day—" He gasped. "One d–day of your—your time. That's—that's all I'm—I'm asking. But—but, please—please don't—don't turn me in," he said as if he could read her mind.

Her stomach clenching with indecision, Angela did something she had not done in years. She shot a brief prayer heavenward, beseeching the Lord to direct her decision. Torn with anxiety, she at last settled upon the first plan. Angela would at least treat this human being with the dignity she had bestowed upon her stray cat. She would give the man water and food and tend his wound. After that, she would face the other decisions to be made.

"Can you walk?" she asked as another doubt nagged her. One of the conditions of her teaching contract involved Angela's not allowing men into her home unless they were escorted.

"M–maybe," he said, relief evident in his relaxing shoulders. "If—if you'll help—help me."

Nervously, Angela looked to the east and noted the sun's position. The children would arrive within an hour. She had precious little time to spare if she was going to successfully hide this man in her home before anyone arrived. No one—*no one* must ever suspect that the Dogwood schoolmistress was housing a lone gentleman. That would mean the end of her job.

"We don't have much time to spare if I'm going to get you settled. I am a schoolteacher. Within the hour, the children will start arriving for school." Leaning on her hoe, Angela grabbed his arm.

"What—what about your h–husband? H–he should— should help."

"Don't have a husband," Angela said in the brusque voice she often used to hide her vulnerability.

"Me either." His irrational comment spoke of his confusion as well as his marital status. And the fact that this desperate human being was also without a wife left her in an even more compromising position.

"Here," she commanded, taking his chilled hand in hers. "Use the hoe handle to pull yourself up." She placed his hand on the hoe, and he gripped it.

After several failed attempts at righting himself, the man dragged himself to his knees. Angela, her pulse pounding, apprehensively glanced across the school yard and up the dusty road. Still, no sign of a living soul. Accompanied by the sound of her rooster's persistent squawking, Angela gritted her teeth and tugged on the man's arm while he stumbled to his feet. Pausing, he gripped the wooden handle with both hands as if it were his lifeline.

"Haven't—haven't eaten since y–yesterday m–morning." He swallowed as if his mouth were full of dust. "N–need some water t–too."

"Yes. . .yes. But, we've got to get you into the house first." Angela stepped to his good side and placed his arm along her shoulders. "Now, lean against me," she commanded, offering her shoulders for support.

"Don't—don't want to knock you o–over, Lady," he said as if he were truly concerned for her safety.

"I'll be fine," she countered with spunk as he relaxed against her. A tall woman, Angela found this man's unusual height a surprise. Many men were shorter than she.

Bit by bit, the pair hobbled out of the garden and toward the cottage. All the while, Angela scanned the yard and surrounding countryside, feeling as if the entire community were watching. But the only eyes observing her belonged to her two horses and the one milk cow, watching them from the north pasture.

The faint smell of leather and horseflesh clung to the man. That, coupled with his warmth, left Angela all too aware that twelve years had lapsed since she had allowed a man this close. Her face flushed with the turn of her thoughts, and she was thankful for the physical exertion that covered any reason for the blush.

As they neared her back door, Angela worriedly glanced over her shoulder to see only the ancient barn and a few hens, pecking here and there. Nonetheless, her feelings of being watched persisted. She glanced toward the face, whose narrow set eyes and long, straight nose reminded her of a Greek sculpture, honed in fine marble. But now, that face blanched with pain. "Are you going to make it?"

"Yes. . .just a few more—more feet," he said through puffing breaths.

Angela, her mind whirling, tried to devise a plan for hiding the man during the next day. The thought of someone finding him in her home and her subsequent dismissal from her job left her wondering if she should reverse her decision and turn him in to the authorities. But Angela recalled the flickering light in his deep. serious eyes. In spite of his condition, the spirit she saw melted her heart and made him seem more like a crippled deer rather than a gunshot murderer.

Nonetheless, the face of Jason Wiley flashed across her mind. *He had beautiful eyes—eyes that made me want to melt*. She dashed a glance at the victim then looked at her back door, only feet away. *I'm crazy!* she thought in panic and coerced herself not to jump away from him. The winds of indecision once more accosted her, like an angry hurricane, yanking a lone ship from one watery, mountainous crest to another. Her pulse pounding all the more urgently, she continued her journey until the back door was within reach. Angela, rigid with fear, stopped in her tracks and stared at the metal doorknob as if it were a coiled copperhead, so prevalent during east Texas summers.

Gasping for air, the man seemed to relinquish a new portion of his weight upon her shoulders with every minute that passed. Her spine and neck aching, Angela fought back the tears of doubt that pushed against her soul. She felt the man's curious appraisal and darted a glance into his eyes. A current of silent communication flashed between them, and Angela voiced her misgivings.

"If anyone finds out I'm hiding you, I'll lose my—my job." She gulped and forced the tears into abeyance. "And—and if you're lying to me, Mister—"

"I'm t–telling you the—the truth," he said feebly, his face seeming to grow more ashen with every word.

Across the yard, that persistent rooster produced another hoarse crow, and Angela jumped. Then, a dove's soft cooing brought back memories of her brother, Eric. Even as a child, he had loved to sit outside and listen to the doves. But Eric was in heaven now. He had arrived at the pearly gates as a young man because he had been falsely accused of a heinous crime. This man, leaning upon her, claimed a similar fate.

Without another thought, she reached for the door-knob, twisted it, and allowed the creaking door to swing inward. As her cat scurried into the kitchen, the sound of the door's unoiled hinges sent a chill across Angela's spirit. She cast another indecisive look at the man and held his tormented gaze. Something in the center of her being shuddered in reaction to his rugged, masculine appeal. Even with his features twisted in pain, this tall man, so close to Angela, left her recalling the nights she had pondered the possibilities of allowing herself to fall in love once more. These unexpected thoughts made Angela want to run all the more.

"P–please, Lady, don't—don't desert m–me now," he stammered as if he could read her mind.

"I have precious little choice at this point," she said with practical resignation, although images of Eric left her feeling far from practical. "I can't exactly leave you sitting on my porch steps." Angela, accepting this very truth herself, placed her foot on the first of three short steps leading up to the back door. "If you can make it into the kitchen, I think I have the perfect spot for you," she said, thinking of the storm cellar underneath the braided rug.

"Oh?" he said, a note of caution in his voice. "D–do you—you plan to—to boil me in—in oil?"

Angela turned widened eyes toward the man to see a spark of humor tilting the corners of tight lips and trailing through his dark, limpid eyes. "No indeed," she answered firmly, refusing to smile. "My father and brothers dug out a storm cellar under the kitchen a year ago after a tornado helped itself to my roof. I keep a mattress, lamp, and bedding down there—just in case."

The two of them struggled up the three wooden steps, only to have the man stumble over the door's threshold and collapse just inside the kitchen. Angela, still firmly holding onto her charge, joined him in a heap on the floor, her knees and right hip stinging with the jolt of the fall.

A low groan erupted from the man.

"I'm sorry," Angela said breathlessly while trying to disentangle herself from his long arms. Her face heating anew, she evaluated the impropriety of her position and ascertained that if the facts concerning the activities of the morning fell into the right hands, she would be unemployed by sundown. Forcing herself to remain calm, she determined to place as much distance as possible between her and this stranger who had been dropped into her life. Angela wrenched the bonnet from her head, cast it aside, stood, and reached for his legs. She swung them into the kitchen and shut the door with a decided click. The shadows that engulfed them seemed the cloak of finality. Angela had made her decision. She hoped she did not live to regret it.

four

Thirty minutes later, Angela stood at the top of the ladder, which led into the storm cellar. She paused, brushing aside the beads of perspiration on her forehead that resulted from her labor and distress. Getting the man down the ladder and onto that mattress had been an adventure, to say the least. Already, Angela felt as if she had worked from sunup to sundown. Darting repeated glances toward the window, she took a deep breath and clutched the mug of herbal tea and extra quilt she planned to deliver to the man. The first pupils had begun to arrive. Soon, they would wonder where she was.

Angela carefully picked her way down the steep steps and into the coolness of the dark earth, illuminated by only the flickering flames of twin candles and the pinpoints of light seeping through the cracks in the kitchen floor. The man lying on the feather mattress amidst the shadows observed her with gentle eyes. "Thanks for the water and soup," he said, his voice and breathing less strained. "I—I think I'm already improving."

Before her last trip to the cellar, Angela had retrieved last night's soup from the spring house. Upon presenting the man with some sustenance, he had attacked both the water and warmed-up soup so ferociously that she made him slow his intake. "I'm glad they helped. I brought you some of Dr. Engle's special tea." She extended the warm mug and he propped himself up to receive it. "He gave it to me last spring when I wrenched my ankle. The tea will help you sleep and take some of the edge off the pain."

As he greedily drank the liquid, Angela moved about in silence, spreading the extra blanket across the man's form. She planned to place a chamber pot in the room before leaving for school, a distasteful, yet necessary task. She felt Noah watching her and that left her all the more uncomfortable. *Oh Lord*, she prayed to herself. *I know I haven't been the best at keeping up between me and You, but if You could just assure me that I haven't made a mistake concerning this man. . .and—and get me out of this situation without anyone discovering what I've done.*

"The children are arriving," she said formally. "I must tend to my duties."

"Yes. . .of course," he said politely as he set the empty mug on the floor beside the bed.

She reached toward the stoneware basin sitting next to the mattress and picked up the white cloth lying in the cool water. The sounds of dripping liquid accompanied her wringing out the makeshift bandage. "I'll remove the other cloth and place this new one on your wound. Hopefully, by the time I come back to check on you, the water will have dissolved all the dried blood and we can get a better idea of how bad off you are. Right now, I think it's just a deep surface wound."

"Hurts like half my side is gone."

"I can only imagine," Angela said. She pulled back the covers and tugged aside the first cloth, already stained red.

He winced and produced a pain-filled gasp.

"Sorry," she said. "I think the bleeding has about stopped altogether, if that makes you feel any better."

"I feel better than—than I have in days," he said as she laid the damp cloth on the wound and replaced the covers.

With the sound of children squealing in the school yard, Angela paused for a moment to search the man's eyes. The appreciation and admiration flowing from his dark orbs left a tendril of respect twining its way through her spirit. An unexpected question scurried through her mind: *Would a convicted criminal be so polite and thankful?*

"I think you just saved my life, Lady," he said, gratitude oozing from his words. "Do you, by chance, have a name?" Again, a faint smile attested to a sense of humor, not far beneath the surface of the pain and drowsiness.

"Miss Isaacs. Miss Angela Isaacs," she replied, never taking her gaze from his. "And yours?"

"Reverend Noah Thorndyke."

Her brows shot up of their own volition.

"Surprised?" he asked, his eyelids drooping. "They think I'm a killer named—named Rupert Denham. It would seem that we look alike. I was scheduled to hang this morning. Instead, looks like I met an angel." He lazily observed Angela.

She flinched as his words brought back unpleasant childhood memories.

"I'm sorry. I have offended you," Noah said with concern.

Sighing, Angela shook her head. "It's nothing. I took no offense." During her school days, some of Angela's classmates had tormented her by dubbing her "Angel." She had always been taller and thinner than the other children and often she was assigned the part of an angel in Christmas plays. Soon, several of the bratty boys had shortened "Angela" to just "Angel." The nickname stuck, especially when her classmates learned she detested the moniker.

The clanging of the school bell announced the arrival of the Johnson twins. Those two third-graders apparently didn't believe they could survive one day without ringing the bell loudly enough to be heard across the county.

"Sounds like they're ready for you," Noah said, eyeing her with a mixture uncertainty, distrust, and fear.

"Yes. I must go now. I'll check on you as soon as I can." Gathering her skirt, Angela stood.

"Please, Miss Angela. Promise me. Promise you won't turn me in?" Noah asked, his face full of apprehension.

Chewing her bottom lip, Angela again debated her predicament. "I could lose *my job* over having you here," she said. "It would be incriminating enough that you are a gentleman. But the fact that, by your own admission, you're a convicted criminal—"

"And innocent. I could lose *my life*." He grimaced as

if the very words increased the pain in his side.

The bell continued its incessant clanging, and Angela moved toward the ladder only a few feet away. She weighed his potent comments. His life was certainly more valuable than her job. *But what if he isn't innocent?* As she gripped the ladder, a new thought struck her. This man said he was a preacher, but could he prove it? She exposed him to a piercing gaze and stated, "Quote the Twenty-third Psalm."

"Excuse me?" He squinted as though he were straining to catch her meaning.

"The Twenty-third Psalm—can you quote it?"

"Yes, but—"

"You say you're a preacher. Do you know your Bible?"'

Immediately, he began to slowly, deliberately, quote the well-known passage.

When he finished, Angela blurted, "What about Genesis 1:1?"

"In the beginning God created the heaven and the earth." He held her gaze and continued, a firm edge to his otherwise sleepy voice. "And the earth was without form, and void; and darkness was upon the face of the waters. And God said, Let there be light; and there was light. And God saw—"

"And can you recite the story of the birth of Jesus from Luke?" Angela asked, now expecting him to meet her request.

His gaze never wavering, he obliged her. Three verses into his recitation, he stumbled across several words and knitted his brows as if the effort were taxing his strength.

"That's fine," Angela said, her voice reflecting her growing distress. If he were indeed telling the absolute truth about his predicament, that left her in a precarious situation. She could not, in good conscience, turn out an innocent man to be hanged. The potential tragedy left her reeling with a new sense of moral obligation. Fresh memories of Eric's cruel death flooded her as Angela chose one last test to prove Noah Thorndyke's Bible knowledge. "And what about Malachi six-twenty?"

"There's—there's no s–such chapter," he said, as if each word required increasing effort.

Something in the deepest recesses of Angela's soul confirmed that the man was very likely telling her the truth. Her chilled fingers, gripping the ladder, shook against the rough wood. The dank smells of earth seemed at once suffocating. The lantern, flickering near Noah's mattress, accented his distraught features. And all Angela could think was, *Dear Lord, what have I gotten myself into?*

The school bell, which had ceased for a season, began ringing all the louder. "I'll be back as soon as possible," she said.

Noah nodded, his eyes closing as if he could no longer hold them open. "And—and you won't—won't tell?" he slurred, but before Angela could answer, his rhythmical breathing attested to sleep's claim.

Her stomach churning, Angela raced up the ladder, and retrieved the chamber pot. After setting it in the corner, she ascended back into the kitchen, closed the cellar door, and covered it with the woven rug. She rushed to her bedroom and examined her appearance in the dresser mirror. A cobweb graced her hair, along the edge of her bun. Dirt smudged her nose. And the expression in her brown eyes spoke of a woman deeply troubled.

Angela schooled her features into her schoolmistress mien, dashed away the cobweb, and stepped to the washbasin. She thoroughly scrubbed her hands and splashed her face with cool water. She dried her face on the way to the kitchen and dropped the cotton cloth on the rough-hewn, oak dining table. When she stepped onto the short back door steps and looked down, Angela spotted the imprints of a man's boots in the dust, near her cottage. Violently trembling, Angela dashed back inside, grabbed her worn broom, and rushed outdoors to brush furiously at the footprints until they were no more.

She propped the broom by the back door and rushed toward the group of mischievous boys gathered around the school bell.

"Teacher! Here comes Teacher," one of them squawked before all raced toward the schoolhouse.

Frowning, Angela followed in their wake, up the short flight of steps, and opened the door leading into the one-room haven of learning that resembled a small chapel. With the change of every season, Angela meticulously changed the schoolroom's look. Through the years, she had collected a wide array of colored material and used it to create an aura pleasing to the senses.

Presently, the walls on either side of the chalkboard were covered with cloth the color of pumpkins. Angela had used the tiny nails that held the material in place to tack leaves and branches of pine needles upon the fabric. The two bookcases, large globe, and printed multiplication tables added to the room's aura of learning.

Presently, all twenty-five of Angela's students rigidly sat in their worn desks, facing the chalkboard. She pondered the necessity of taking the boys to task over the bell ringing but decided not to. Given all that had happened this morning, Angela had precious little strength left to chide children, despite their deserving it.

"Let's get our morning underway," she said, briskly stepping into the schoolroom. She started to close the door behind her but hesitated as the sound of horses' hooves pounded into the school yard. Angela, glancing over her shoulder, caught sight of one symbol amidst the flurry of horses: a sheriff's badge. Approximately twelve men accompanied a lawman, whose scowl spoke of hours in the saddle and a determination to accomplish his goal.

Immediately, Angela realized the men were looking for the person under her kitchen floor. Feeling as if she would lose her breakfast, Angela barked out the commands to her students. "First graders, work on your alphabet and making capital letters. Alex, you and Jenny call out the multiplication tables to each other. Grades six and seven have reading assignments. Grades eight and nine, study your world maps; there will be a test on European countries this afternoon. Lea Ann, read over your essay and check for any errors. I want to go over the grammar with you in a few minutes. Now, did I miss anyone?" No hands went up. "All right, everyone, busy now!"

Behind her, a faint knock on the door, which still stood ajar, sent a compulsive jump through Angela. Although she had fully expected one of the men to approach, his presence seemed to bring with him images of Noah Thorndyke. She turned to stare up into the sheriff's intense, gray eyes that suggested he tolerated no compromise. Under a dark, bushy mustache, his lips drew into a tight line. A bright, silver star occupied a prominent place on the pocket of his black vest.

"Yes, may I help you?" Angela asked, relying on her years of experience at maintaining composure under the direst of circumstances.

"Mornin', ma'am," the lawman offered. "May I have a moment of your time?"

"Of course," Angela said. "Children, I am closing this door momentarily, but I will be right on the other side. I don't want to hear a peep from any of you." They dutifully continued their work. Angela, her throat constricting so tightly she could hardly breathe, stepped onto the top step and closed the door behind her. She knew before the lawman ever spoke what his inquiry would consist of, and she had no idea how she would answer.

"I'm Sheriff Garner from Rusk. We're out lookin' for this criminal." With that persistent rooster crowing from Angela's yard, the sheriff held up a wanted poster.

Angela examined the poster to discover the almost exact image of the man who now lay under her kitchen floor. The same dark, heavy brows. The same close-set eyes. The same prominent nose and square jawline. The name "Rupert Denham" was printed under the likeness.

Her mind whirling with a fresh onslaught of misgivings, Angela relived the events of the morning up until minutes ago when Noah Thorndyke told her they thought he was Rupert Denham.

"Have you seen a rider bearing this resemblance pass here in the last couple of hours? We're chasin' this killer. He's dangerous. He broke out of jail by duping my deputy with card tricks. We found his horse 'bout a mile up the road, near a stream."

Angela, gulping in fear, glanced toward the group of men in the school yard. Their grim faces bore the identical question, the same determination, the certainty that they would snare their prey. Angela's face chilled with the implications of her predicament. Within the last hour, she had broken her teacher's contract and possibly housed a criminal. *What must I have been thinking?* Nervously, she toyed with the watch hanging around her neck.

"Don't mean to scare you none, now, ma'am," the sheriff said, his voice softening. At last remembering his manners, the lawman removed his hat and held it at his side as if he were attempting to hide the imposing Colt Peacemaker attached to his hip. "We're just trying to do our job. And it's very likely that there's a dangerous killer in your area. If you happen to see him. . ." Pausing, the sheriff gazed across the countryside, and Angela remembered the dried blood on the weeds in her garden.

She opened her mouth, ready to do what she should have done when she first saw the sheriff—blurt the location of Rupert Denham. But some insistent impression deep within her soul stopped the words before they left her lips. The man in the cellar said his name was really Noah Thorndyke. *Reverend* Noah Thorndyke. His quoting of scripture had even backed his claims of being a preacher. Most killers could not quote scripture like Noah had—but, then again, most preachers did not skillfully play with cards. And, Sheriff Garner had said he tricked the deputy with cards.

Her palms sweating profusely, Angela rubbed them against the sides of her skirt and licked her lips. *Dear God, what do I say?* she pleaded, feeling the sheriff's scrutiny. Lips quivering, Angela could only stare at the image on the wanted poster and flounder for a proper response while tears of anxiety blurred her eyes.

"Ma'am, it looks like I've scared you out of a year's growth," Garner said. "Wasn't my intent. But you and the children need to be mighty careful. Might not even hurt to close the school down for the day—just 'til we can find our man. This rat killed a banker in our town, and he was supposed to be hanged and dead by now. So he's desperate to get away. I wouldn't put it past him to kill or cheat or lie. . .whatever he has to do to get out of facing that rope he deserves."

Lie. . .lie. . .lie. . . The word echoed through Angela's mind like a chant, bent on proving Noah Thorndyke really was Rupert Denham. She opened her mouth to disclose the truth, but once more, that insistence deep in her soul stayed her words. "I'll send all the children home," she said.

"Good idea, Miss. . ."

"Isaacs. Miss Angela Isaacs." Keeping her eyes downcast, Angela extended her hand, hoping the sheriff interpreted her demure actions as those of a lady, following the rules of propriety.

"If you can round up your young 'uns quick-like, I'll get my men to escort them home."

"Yes. . .yes, of course," Angela agreed, relieved to be free of her duties. The upheaval of the morning had left her so addled, she felt anything but capable of teaching a room full of children. Furthermore, she wasn't certain a man in Noah Thorndyke's condition needed to be left to his own upkeep for the duration of a school day. He would need more water and food. In her haste, Angela had left no extra provisions for the man who claimed to be innocent.

She opened the door wider, and extended a hand for the sheriff to enter. Turning on her heel, Angela walked to the front of the classroom and faced them. "Children, there has been a turn of events in our day," she said succinctly. "It seems there is a man at large who might be a danger to us. Sheriff Garner and his men have offered to escort each of you to your homes."

A collective gasp went up from the children. As one, they turned toward the sheriff, towering in the back of the schoolroom.

"Are they looking for a murderer?" Lea Ann Turner asked. At fourteen, Lee Ann seemed more a young lady than a schoolgirl and her questions usually reflected the intuitions of a full-grown woman.

"That's neither here nor there, children," Angela snapped, not wanting to alarm her students any more than they would be under such odd circumstances. Besides, Angela well knew where the supposed convict resided and thoroughly believed the students were not in danger. However, she also knew she must behave in a logical manner with the sheriff; it was logical for a schoolteacher to allow her students to be escorted home. "Now, all of you gather your things and do as Sheriff Garner tells you." Gripping her hands behind her, Angela leaned back against her oversized desk ever so slightly—just enough to maintain her balance. Otherwise, she was certain her knocking knees would buckle beneath her at any given moment.

The students, bustling with excitement, grabbed their books and papers and hats and approached the sheriff. Angela, calling out instructions for proper conduct, followed in their wake. In a matter of minutes, the sheriff and Angela had assigned the sheriff's twelve men to their respective children and given out directions to the children's homes. Angela, hovering near the bottom step, watched as the children frolicked toward their homes, the horsemen close beside. Squeals of delight erupted across the countryside, belying the gravity of the moment.

Feigning composure, Angela compressed her lips and

nodded toward the sheriff, standing nearby. After a brief thank you, she walked up the short flight of steps and back into the schoolroom. The smell of chalk and musty books enveloped her, and at once seemed the stifling pall of accusation. Angela rushed toward her meticulous desk, plopped into her straight-backed chair, propped her elbows atop her hand-made desk calendar, and covered her face with her hands. Every nerve in her body quivered in reaction to the mammoth problem that lay before her. With every passing minute that Angela did not speak the truth to the sheriff, she dug herself deeper and deeper into the pit of Noah Thorndyke's predicament. If anyone learned the truth of what she had done that morning, she would most certainly lose her job and probably every scrap of her flawless reputation.

For some reason, the image of Jason Wiley swam before her mind's eye. That man had been nothing but a lying, two-faced womanizer who looked as innocent as a lamb. He could also quote numerous scriptures from memory and produced enough "amens" during Sunday morning worship to impress most the countryside. In light of Jason's convincing performance, Angela wondered if she had been a fool to let Noah Thorndyke's knowledge of scripture influence her into actually believing him. She had trusted one man and vowed never to trust again. *Have I lost my mind?*

Noah's dark, honest eyes, like twin pools of ink, flashed through her mind. His tousled hair, the color of teak. His square jaw, shadowed with need of a shave.

His insistence that he was innocent blended with memories of the man's masculine appeal. Noah Thorndyke was by no means as handsome as that Jason had been, but he had pulled at Angela's heart from almost the moment she saw him, helplessly lying in her garden.

Perhaps Angela's years as a spinster had finally caught up with her. For, despite her vows of avoiding all men, her lonely heart now seemed to be making decisions for her.

Angela Isaacs was lonely. Yes, lonely. She had never admitted that truth to a living soul. And even pondering the reality this morning left her traitorously wanting to walk back to her home and check on the man in the cellar. She shook her head in disgust, defeat, and distress. *If you are not guilty, Noah Thorndyke, then my helping you is the only honorable choice. But if you really are a murderer, then I am the biggest fool in Texas.*

The sound of the school door's opening interrupted her thoughts, and a quick upward glance confirmed the worst: Sheriff Garner had returned. His hat in hand, he speculatively observed Angela. Although a good twenty feet separated them, Angela felt as if his keen, gray eyes bore into her very soul. The suspenseful silence that settled around them seemed to drop a bucket full of cold, jagged rocks into Angela's stomach.

"Sorry to bother you again, Ma'am," the sheriff said in a measured voice. "But I just wanted to say that. . . let's just say a young woman were to happen to find that criminal and were to think of helpin' him. . ." He paused as if he were carefully considering every word.

". . .The penalty for such ain't really appropriate for a lady like yourself."

"Sheriff, *please*," Angela gasped, so shocked she could think of nothing else to say.

The conviction in Garner's eyes wavered, and he glanced at the wooden floor. "Sorry, ma'am," the tall lawman said. Squinting, he looked back at Angela as if he were still gauging her response. "It's just that one of my men had to get off his horse and chase after them twin boys. They ran into your garden, and my deputy came back to say he seen some blood near your dried up corn stalks. I went over there, and the weeds are pressed down like somebody's been layin' in 'em."

Her face growing cold, Angela stared wide-eyed at the lawman. She had absolutely no words to respond to the man's direct inquiry. *Dear God, help me!* was all her mind could conjure.

Garner, a brawny man with hands the size of bear paws, cleared his throat as if he were highly uncomfortable with Angela's scrutiny. She had witnessed the exact same response out of more than one overbearing father, thwarted in his attempts to intimidate his son's teacher. "I suppose. . .I've jumped to a wrong conclusion. There's always the likelihood that an injured deer spent the night in your garden. I don't suppose that a lady in your position—"

"Thank you, Sheriff," Angela said firmly. Standing on wobbly legs, she did what she had done throughout her teaching career. Angela, sensing she had gained her bluff, took every measure to maintain the advantage in this interaction. She placed her palms against the top of the desk, drew upon every scrap of composure she could muster, and observed the overgrown sheriff as if he were a truant schoolboy.

"Would you like me to escort you somewhere?" he asked, as if he were genuinely sorry for his assumptions.

"No. . .no, that's all right," Angela supplied evenly. Straightening, she rearranged the neat row of pencils on her desk. "I have work to do here and in my home." *As in, deciding what I'm going to do about Noah Thorndyke.* "And I can securely lock the schoolroom and my cottage. I, um, also know how to use my papa's old shotgun if the occasion arises."

"Well, we've already given this area a good lookin' over. Even if he *did* spend the night in your garden, I'd say he has moved along."

Choosing not to respond, Angela held the lawman's gaze as he nervously fingered his Peacemaker then hedged his way toward the door. "Mighty nice makin' your acquaintance, ma'am," he said with a nod before taking his leave.

When the door clicked shut, Angela expelled her pent-up breath and collapsed back into the chair.

five

For hours, Noah drifted between the awareness of the dank, dimly lit cellar and the sensation of lying encased in a tomb. The dull pain in his side seemed a mere remnant of the sharp tormentor it had been. However, Noah tossed on the mattress, encased in the grips of sporadic and fitful slumber. Scenes from his youth played in the shadows of his mind like vague specters of the past. Images came and stood in the distance, their edges blurred and colors distorted, running together in whirlpools surging to the center. He strained to hear the voices but their whispers only tantalized his ears with sketches of familiarity.

Once he thought his mother passed by. She appeared to hold out her arms and call to him, but the words were garbled; then she was gone. How he wished to speak to her and explain—no, ask forgiveness for leaving home, breaking her heart. Yet, even in his confusion, Noah remembered a time when he had already done exactly that. . .

. . .Then the phantom of a huge raft floating in a shoreless river moved toward him. The deck held scores of men—brawling and cursing—trying to grab Noah while the ship glided by. As the stern

came abreast of Noah, a man in a long coat and
beaver hat held up a pair of dice and a deck of
cards. He dropped the pack and turned to a black
and red wheel behind him. Thousands of numbers
dotted its surface. Noah grasped the side of the
boat and tried to pull himself aboard. But the well-
dressed man stomped his hands and spat on him,
mumbling in derision of the boy's skills. Guns
barked. The gambler fell into the water, dragging
Noah with him. The boy fought for air; then everything went black. . .

But from the pits of that blackness came the faint
smell of warm wax, the feel of a soft, homespun quilt,
the distant caw of a crow. With great effort, Noah
allowed his eyelids to admit the tiniest bit of light. The
yellow glow from candles burning on a ledge across the
room gave a momentary illusion of sunrise. He fully
opened his eyes and surveyed the dark corners of his
cell. As in his muddled dreams, Noah's mind raced
with panicked thoughts that perhaps he was in a
tomb—buried alive after a failed hanging. Desperately,
he glanced from side to side in hopes of discovering his
location. The erratic dance of the flames only increased
the tomb's eeriness and Noah's heart violently thudded.
    Then, Noah remembered. . .he remembered a
woman, tall and lithe, with hair the color of chestnuts
and brown eyes as soft as the velvet coat of a newborn
colt. Angela—her name was Angela. For some reason,
she did not like his calling her an angel. Relaxing,

Noah closed his eyes and the faint sound of a woman's footsteps above him increased his feeling of security. Before the doctor's tea gained control once more, Noah reminded himself that he owed that angel his life. . .

. . .Yet, again, a dreary plodding dream overtook Noah's mental images, and his steps led to a cottage deep in a grove of massive oaks. The roof tilted in a steep angle and grew spots of green moss on the south side. The walls were half river stones and whitewashed above. A mirror hung on the wall, and on the lawn a child played in front of the mirror. He rolled a ball in a tight circle with his foot. But another child in the mirror attempted to chase the ball and kick it away. Repeatedly the boy on the lawn laughed and called to the other to come out of the mirror and play with him. But the mirror child frowned and doubled his fists, then turned away. Thunder rumbled in the distance and a cool breeze blew across the landscape. Suddenly a light burst against the horizon, momentarily distracting Noah. As the light continued its soft glow, a voice called his name several times.

He opened his eyes and squinted. The angel stood before him—the woman who had said her name was Angela Isaacs. Behind her, the cellar door emitted a wide shaft of light. In her hands, she held a tray of food that smelled as if it came straight from the corridors of heaven. The light from the door and the candlelight, flickering behind her, created a halo effect around her disheveled hair. Her ethereal image left the groggy Noah wondering exactly how long her tresses were and exactly how they would feel beneath his touch.

"I'm glad to see you're awake," Angela said quietly, her soft eyes kind yet worried. "It's almost two in the afternoon. You've been asleep since this morning when I left."

"Are you through with your school duties?" Noah asked as the memories of his predicament plopped into his mind, piece by piece.

"Yes." She knelt beside him, placed the tray on the floor, and busied herself with the arranging of dishes filled with food. "The sheriff arrived first thing this morning, saying he was looking for a convicted criminal named Rupert Denham." Pausing, Angela exposed him to a gaze full of fear and questions.

A tight knot as cold as a gun barrel formed in the pit of Noah's stomach. His tongue thick, he swallowed against a throat dry from sleep.

"And?" he asked nervously.

"He suggested that his men escort the children home, and I let him," she finished.

"So, you didn't—"

"No." She shook her head. "Not a word."

The knot in his stomach dissolved. "Thank God," he breathed.

"Do you feel like you can sit up and eat?" she asked, avoiding eye contact. "I have a small stool I can bring down to sit the tray on."

"Yes, thank you," Noah said, attempting to put as much honor and respect into those three little words as humanly possible. "I owe you my life," he added, repeating the sentiment he had already expressed before his long slumber.

As if she were overwrought with the burden of her charge, Angela's lips trembled and she produced but a faint nod. "How's your side?" she asked, standing.

"Better. . .thanks to you."

"Good," she said simply. Turning toward the pair of candles on the ledge, she removed a fresh taper from her apron pocket and replaced one of the spent candles.

Noah, gazing up at her, decided that Miss Angela Isaacs was by far the most enchanting specimen of femininity that he had ever encountered. The gentle turn of her lips and the hint of vulnerability in her eyes coupled with her spirit's serenity and strength began to render Noah almost giddy with the magnitude of his good fortune. Somehow, the Reverend Noah Thorndyke had gotten himself sentenced to hang, then escaped from jail, and landed in the hands of a woman of virtue who had snatched his life from the jaws of death. And the thought that sprang upon him left him breathless: *Is this whole predicament the product of good fortune or the result of God's handiwork?* His mind rushed back to the night before he left on his journey from Louisiana into East Texas. That very night, Noah had prayed that God would somehow use the trip as a means to provide him a wife, a suitable helpmate for his ministry. *Could it be?* he mused, then dashed aside the notion.

At once, Noah forced himself to turn his thoughts away from such alarming and unlikely matters. He had other concerns besides the woman whose skirts produced a delightful swish as she ascended the ladder. His life was in jeopardy!

Abruptly, Noah propped himself up on his elbow, only to produce a moan of protest when his wounded side complained. Angela immediately postponed her upward journey and rushed to his side. Kneeling nearby, she placed her arm behind Noah's shoulders to lend support while she stuffed an extra feather pillow beneath his shoulder blades. Noah, enveloped in a sweet, floral scent, observed Angela's concerned face and wondered if her cheeks were as soft as they appeared. His gut clenched, and he decided not to tell her that he felt capable of sitting up alone, despite the protest in his stiff side.

"Is that better?" she asked, trying to pull away from him. But something stopped her short, and she produced a frustrated groan as she looked downward. Noah followed her gaze to see that the chain of the watch she wore around her neck had somehow tangled in a button on his shirt. Her fingers shaking, she tried to maneuver the chain, but only tangled it worse.

"Here, let me help you," Noah said as she fumbled with his button. He reached for the chain, but instead found his fingers closing around her hands. Her trembling fingers stilled within his grasp. Noah's gaze slowly traveled up her arm, across her shoulder, and found refuge in the softness of her brown eyes, as tender as an adolescent's when she's courted by her first beau.

A thrill of attraction zipped through Noah and re-flected itself in Angela's eyes. His reaction, so confus-ing and unexpected, left him breathless with its potency. Noah's focus, bent on betraying him, trailed to her quiv-ering lips. The inappropriate desire to kiss this woman surged through him, and he severely restrained himself with memories of his profession.

As if Angela could read his every thought, she pressed her lips together, disentangled her hands from his, gripped the chain, and ripped it away from his shirt, dis-lodging the button in its wake. Standing, she spun on her heel and marched back toward the ladder. "I'll return shortly with your stool," Angela ground out. Her words, as cold as jagged rocks, left Noah with no questions about her disapproval.

"Please don't be angry with me, Miss Isaacs. I guess—I guess—you saved my life," he repeated the amazing truth. "I think it's most natural for a man to. . . to feel grateful and. . .and want to express that."

Her back to him, Angela paused at the ladder, as if she were waiting for his further words. However, the sound of someone knocking on a door penetrated the cellar, and a woman's muffled voice called out Angela's name.

She gasped and whirled to face Noah. "That sounds like my cousin, Rachel." Her eyes wide with apprehen-sion, she peered at Noah as a silent, panicked communi-cation flashed between them. "Do the best you can to eat your meal. I know you must be hungry, but eat *quietly*.

I'll check on you as soon as I get rid of—um, I mean, as soon as Rachel leaves."

"Yes, please do," Noah said with a faint smile. Perhaps his own precarious predicament was leaving him delirious, but Angela's bluntly saying she would "get rid of" her own cousin left Noah responding with humor. Her matronly scowl, obviously meant to put him—and *keep* him—in his place, only increased Noah's grin.

After a final glare, Angela tromped up the ladder, and climbed into the kitchen. Noah's perverse humor demanded that he release a faint chuckle. Before closing the cellar door, she produced a glower fierce enough to stop a rabid bull in his tracks. "There is absolutely nothing funny about this," she hissed. "You're a wanted man, and I'm an accessory. Do you have any idea what will happen if you're caught in my house? My reputation and my job will be ruined."

"Angela? It's Rachel! Are you here?" the feminine voice called again.

"I'm sorry, ma'am," Noah said as meekly as he could. "No harm intended. It's just that—well, if you don't mind my saying, you are a sight when you're riled."

"Yes, that's what they tell me," she whispered, her eyes glaring bullets at him. Without another word, Angela lowered the cellar door, and left Noah to his own devises.

Yes, you're a sight, Miss Isaacs. A sight for sore eyes. A beautiful sight, indeed. The vision of an angel. Noah reached for his food tray and scooted it closer.

Weak with apprehension, emotional fatigue, and a blazing dose of ire, Angela quietly closed the door in the floor. Within seconds, she scooted the woven rug over the door and strategically placed one of the pine dining chairs atop the rug. Rachel produced another round of knocks, and Angela blindly brushed at her disheveled hair, hoping there were no cobwebs gracing her locks.

She rushed the few feet across the tiny cottage's parlor to open the front door and find a worried Rachel looking at her in exasperation. "You scared me to death, Angel. I thought he'd already gotten you!"

"Who?" Angela asked, wondering if Rachel would *ever* stop calling her Angel.

The petite redhead turned and waved to a man sitting on the driver's bench of the work wagon. "I don't have but a minute," Rachel said, brushing past Angela. "Travis is at home with Little Trav. We decided I needed to come get you and Travis wouldn't hear of my coming alone, considering the escaped criminal that's on the loose. So he sent one of the hired hands with me. He would have come himself, but we decided that I'd have a better chance of getting you to come home with us, considering your stubborn streak—" Her pale brown eyes widening, Rachel covered her lips and stared up at her cousin while a silent "oops" seemed to ricochet around the room.

Angela bit her lips to stop the burst of laughter that threatened to spew forth. Apparently, Noah's warped sense of humor had rubbed off on her. Or perhaps the desire to laugh was just a way to expend some of the emotions that had churned through Angela since she found Noah in her garden. At once, she understood Noah's own chuckles and immediately forgave his inappropriate humor. He must be under more pressure than Angela could ever imagine. Even though her job was at stake, Noah's life was on the line. If Sheriff Garner found him, Angela had no questions that the lawman would execute his immediate hanging.

"I'm sorry," Rachel said after the weighty, lengthy pause. "I didn't mean to. . ." Rachel nervously rubbed the band of freckles that had claimed her nose since childhood—freckles, so like Angela's.

"It's okay," Angela said over a chuckle. "You're right. I'm as stubborn as a mule—at least that's what Papa always says. But then, so are you," Angela said, pointing her finger at Rachel's upturned nose. The cousins shared companionable laughter.

Although Angela was a full decade older than her younger cousin, the two had been close friends since Rachel's adolescence—a friendship which deepened after Rachel experienced a miscarriage and the Lord provided a redheaded newborn for them to adopt. But while the cousins shared the same stubborn streak, their personalities varied. Rachel had always been more spontaneous while Angela was more certain, thoughtful, and precise. Other than their similar coloring of red hair, freckles, and skin tone, their appearance contrasted as widely as their personalities. While Rachel was petite and cute, Angela had always been ganglier and in her opinion, plain, despite the glow of admiration she had seen in the eyes of more than one man.

Angela tried to make up for her lack of classic beauty with an air of composure and dignity. That demeanor reaped respect from her pupils and their parents. *What would they all think if they knew I was housing a criminal?* Angela's strained mind raced in panic.

Rachel produced a resigned sigh as she nervously rubbed her hands against her full skirt. "I came to take you home with me. Are you going to come? Travis and I are really worried about you here by yourself. If you would just consider coming to the ranch, we—"

"No," Angela said gently but firmly. "Earlier this morning, Papa and Mamma sent one of their hired hands for the same reason, but I've chosen to stay here. I have schoolwork to catch up on, and I am perfectly safe. That criminal has probably holed up somewhere by now, anyway." *And you just don't know how truthful that statement really is,* Angela thought as a new surge of irrational laughter bubbled up within her. Images of Noah lying only feet away and undoubtedly hearing every word left Angela feeling as if her features must scream "guilty." That realization dashed aside every nuance of laughter.

"Listen, Angel—"

"I really wish you'd stop calling me Angel," Angela snapped, reacting from the overwhelming agitation that coursed through her veins.

Taken aback by her cousin's sudden rudeness, Rachel once more stared up at Angela in round-eyed scrutiny.

"I'm s–so sorry. I didn't—didn't realize you disliked being called that. I've always thought of it as an endearment of sorts." Rachel's limpid eyes reflected her affected feelings, and Angela felt like a shrew.

"I'm sorry I snapped at you," she said, placing a consoling hand on her cousin's shoulder. "Really. . .it's just that. . ." *It's just that there's a man hiding in my cellar. A man who says he's innocent. A man who I just had the most shameful desire to kiss. I'm overwrought, to say the least.* But Angela voiced none of these thoughts. Instead, she silently appraised her younger cousin who eyed her as oddly as if she had just sprouted spiraling horns from the top of her head.

"Are you feeling all right?" Rachel inquired delicately. "You look a bit pale and. . .and maybe overworked. If there's something I can do for you. . ."

"No. . . No. . ." Angela, forever honest, had never been good at duplicity, and the pressure of her situation left her feeling as if a band of deceit were forever tightening around her heart. Inch by precarious inch, Angela Isaacs was being dragged ever deeper into the pit of Noah Thorndyke's predicament.

Like the grinding jaws of a trap, a new rush of panic clamped onto her soul. Angela's family trusted her. Her students trusted her. Her neighbors trusted her. Yet, she was breaking their faith by housing a convicted murderer.

Images of Noah Thorndyke, with his honest face and gentle, cultured voice, invaded her thoughts. He said he was innocent. With every hour that progressed, Angela became more convinced that he was indeed telling her the truth. For some unexplained reason, she was slowly doing what she had vowed never again to do—trust the word of a man.

Awkwardly, Rachel cleared her throat. "Well. . . ," she said as if she were at a total loss for words. "I guess then, that's your answer." She reached for Angela's arm. "If there's anything I can do—I guess I'm trying to say that, whatever it is that's bothering you—you know I'm here for you."

"I know," Angela said, covering her cousin's hand with hers. "I know."

Clearly troubled, Rachel reluctantly left the cottage. Angela heartily waved at her cousin as her work wagon rolled away, up the dusty road lined with pines. The emotions tumbling through Angela left her teary with relief, with anxiety, with a deeper awareness of the magnitude of her assisting Noah Thorndyke.

Stifling several telltale sniffles, Angela stumbled into the parlor, collapsed onto the velvet settee, and covered her face with her shaking hands. "Oh Lord," she breathed as a new rush of panic swept through her soul. "What have I gotten myself into? You've got to help me." Instinctively, Angela reached for the worn Bible lying atop a doily on the walnut end table near the settee. She had placed the Bible beside the shaded oil lamp as part of the decor of the meticulous home. Angela knew that the sight of the Word of God, so prominent in a teacher's parlor, brought a sense of comfort to any parent who might frequent her quarters.

But only Angela knew that the Bible was there for appearances. Over the years, she had allowed one thing and then another to crowd out her time with the Lord. Furthermore, the various heartaches of life, including Jason Wiley's breach of faith and her brother's unfair death, had somehow seemed a direct betrayal from her Lord.

But this afternoon, Angela was more desperate than she had ever been in her life. Only feet away, beneath the floor of her petite kitchen, lay a convicted criminal, eating a meal Angela had prepared for him. Distraught for some comfort, Angela turned to Proverbs. If ever she needed Solomon's heavenly wisdom, it was today. Even after all the years of not reading the Word as she should, Angela still knew her Bible well. Her mother had made certain that all her children held a solid knowledge of the Word of God.

Hungrily, Angela read the scripture, searching for any phrase or thought, no matter how minuscule, that would bequeath her equilibrium. Upon arriving at Proverbs 3, Angela's gaze fell upon verses five and six. *Trust in the Lord with all thine heart; and lean not unto thine own understanding. In all thy ways acknowledge him, and he shall direct thy paths.* A rush of tingles swept up Angela's spine, leaving her breathless in its wake. A new surge of tears, accompanied by a muffled sob and ample sniffles, preceded the questions that bombarded her soul. *How long has it been since I trusted the Lord with my whole heart? How long since I leaned upon His understanding? How long since I acknowledged Him in all my ways?*

The disturbing questions left Angela reeling with their impact. Immediately, she snapped the Bible shut and plopped it back in its spot on the table. Rising, she took three steps toward the kitchen then stopped, as if she had come against a wall of stone. Only feet away lay a man whose life rested in her hands. He said he was innocent, and his dark, liquid eyes suggested he was telling the truth. Angela thought of her younger brother, Eric, of the night he had been shot and killed by an angry, drunken father who accused him of the worst kind of indecency against his daughter. Months later, Eric's name had been cleared, but that was too late. Eric had already lost his life because of a lie, and by the time the father could have been held account-able, he had died in a drunken stupor. Only three years had passed since that wretched ordeal, and having Noah Thorndyke dropped into her life repeatedly brought those images back, with the full weight of their tragedy.

"Miss Isaacs?" the soft, masculine voice floating from beneath her kitchen left Angela biting her bottom lip. "Miss Isaacs," Noah called again, concern in his voice. "Is everything all right up there?"

Angela walked toward the braided rug in her kitchen. She dashed it aside, and inserted her fingers into the hole shaped like a half-moon. However, she stopped before pulling upward on the cellar door. The last time she was with Noah Thorndyke her chain had caught in his button and he had looked at her with a longing that

Angela had felt many times. A longing to end her lone-liness. A longing to be embraced by that special some-one. Over the years, when those desires came upon Angela, she forced herself to remember Jason Wiley and her vow never to trust again. But now, Angela could not quite decide if that vow had been a wise one.

"Miss Isaacs?" Noah called once more.

Angela lifted the cellar door to see Noah standing at the base of the ladder, clutching it as if he were about to collapse.

"You shouldn't be up," Angela scolded, rushing down the steep steps toward him.

When she stood at his side, Noah observed her with a worried expression. "I thought I heard you crying," he said like a true gentleman.

Guiltily, Angela rubbed the corner of one eye. "I was just—just overwhelmed with the pressure of my en-counter with Rachel."

"I heard everything," Noah said, the flickering can-dles making his pained face seem all the paler. "Thank you so much. There's no way I can ever repay you—and you don't even know me. . ."

"Yes, I have had similar thoughts," Angela said dryly, nudging him toward his mattress. "I see you enjoyed your meal." She nodded toward the empty dishes on the tray as he lowered himself onto his bed.

"Every bite of it." Noah looked up at her as if he were an adolescent boy who had developed an outra-geous attachment to his teacher.

Her cheeks warming, Angela busied herself with the

tray. Schooling her face into a firm mask, she picked up the tray and turned toward the ladder. Despite her better judgment, Noah's blatant admiration left a warm rush of pleasure sprouting from her midsection. She should not—*should not*—react in such a way to a man she just met, and especially a man with a more than questionable background. The memory of her chain getting caught in his button once more wove its way through her mind and left Angela remembering her own shameful desires. She had lived a life of solitude too long—simply too long—and her emotional solitude had left her vulnerable, despite her better judgment.

"So, have you decided whether or not you really believe me yet?" Noah asked softly.

Angela stopped, and the various dishes rattled. "That's neither here nor there," she mumbled over her shoulder before balancing herself on the bottom step.

"Wouldn't you like the details of my predicament before making your final decision?"

The word "no" posed itself on Angela's lips, but she failed to voice it. Instead, her mind whirled with curiosity. Silently, she walked up several steps and slid the wooden tray onto the kitchen floor then descended the ladder once more. Adjusting her skirts, Angela sat on one of the ladder rungs and scrutinized Mr. Thorndyke with a ponderous gaze. "Yes, I think that would be good," she said seriously.

six

Noah silently observed Angela and noted that she seemed to appear more disheveled with every passing moment. The dark circles under her red-rimmed eyes attested to her emotional and physical exhaustion, and Noah hated to think that he was the cause of such distress. But really, he had no choice but to throw himself upon her mercy. As much as he disliked bringing discomfort to a lady of Angela's quality, Noah's desire to escape a hangman's rope proved the most eminent concern.

"I will begin by saying that I believe that God brought me to you. I'm praying that He has a plan to see me through this alive, and I think perhaps you are the instrument He intends to use."

"Are you *really* a preacher?" she blurted. Her fingers, nervously picking at her heavy cotton skirt, revealed her increasing agitation.

"Yes." Noah held her gaze, determined to beam forth an expression of consummate honesty. "When all this happened, I was on my way to Tyler as a candidate for pastor at a congregational church."

"But Sheriff Garner mentioned your tricking the jailer with cards and you even talked about gambling in your sleep," she said, a faint edge of accusation to her words.

The light, spilling through the opened cellar door, highlighted her coppery locks and flushed cheeks, and Noah recalled the long hours when he had beseeched the Lord for a companion. *Could it be?* The question nibbled at the corners of his mind and left him a bit flustered. The moment her watch chain tangled itself in his shirt button flashed through Noah's mind, leaving in its wake the inappropriate longing to feel his lips upon hers.

Noah disciplined himself to keep his thoughts on the issues at hand, on her searching gaze, which seemed to probe the corridors of his mind in quest of the absolute truth. Shifting uncomfortably, Noah debated whether he should tell Angela of his past. Even among his close friends, he had yet to become completely comfortable with relating the story of his rebellion against godly parents, of his sinful past, of his own running from God. Noah had just met this lady and certainly was gripped in the talons of discomfort in relating such intimate, although ghastly, details. However, these wretched circumstances certainly insisted upon levels of intimacy that would normally be considered highly unsuitable. And something in the recesses of Noah's soul suggested that if he expected this angel to continue ministering to him, she needed the whole miserable story, a story that must start at the beginning.

"My parents tell me that when I was about three, they found me one Sunday morning, crying on their doorstep. Around my neck was tied a piece of paper with only the name, 'Noah,' written on it." He intently studied the texture of the dirt walls as he spoke. "I was really sick and they weren't sure I was even going to live. But soon, my health returned, and they realized nobody was coming back for me. After several months, they decided to legally adopt me, but I don't remember any of that. Every memory I have is wrapped up in the parents who raised me. I have no idea what might have happened to cause me to arrive on their porch. But, I do know that my mother had been praying so desperately for a baby. She and my father had been married fifteen years at that time, and she has told me over and over again that I was her special gift from God."

"So you were adopted," Angela mused.

Noah nodded.

"My cousin who was just here—Rachel Isaacs—and her husband adopted a baby boy two years ago."

"I think adoption is a good thing," Noah said. "But then, I guess I would naturally think so." A vague smile played at his lips as images of the strange, plaguing dream again filled his mind. The cottage, deep in a grove of massive oaks. The boy, playing in front of a mirror. The conflict between the child in the mirror and the "real" boy. Recalling the dream made Noah feel as though he swam in a sea of confusion, and he was hard-pressed to maintain his concentration.

He closed his eyes as fresh sorrow issued from his soul. "I told you about my parentage to underscore just how wretched my choices were. Everything my parents did for me makes what I did to them all the more detestable. By the time I was thirteen, I decided I was tired of hearing about the Bible. My father is a Methodist minister who doesn't mince any words when it comes to the Word of God.

"Anyway. . . ," he slowly continued, placing his hand between the pillow and his head. "I ran away from home one night after my father had thoroughly thrashed me."

"Was he terribly mean to you?" Angela asked, a hint of concern in her voice.

"No. I had it coming," Noah replied practically. "And that's the only time I can remember Father really tearing into me. But by that time, I was taller than my mother and, in my father's absence, I had looked down on her and told her just how smart I was and how ignorant she was. When my father came home and found my mother crying. . ." Noah left the rest unsaid. Although twenty years had passed since that pivotal day, his gut tightened with the memory of his own youthful stupidity. He stared up at the kitchen floor with its slits of light seeping into the cellar and thanked God he had come to his senses. "I guess my story is the prodigal son's all over again," he continued. "After I ran away, I wound up living on the Mississippi—gambling, stealing—doing whatever I had to do to survive. That's where I learned how to handle cards," he said, eyeing Angela to gauge her response.

Silently, she observed him, her expression schooled into a bland mask. Feeling as if he were on trial all over again, Noah continued, "I was out in the world about five years when I came to my senses and crawled back home. My parents welcomed me back with opened arms. . .so did God," he added, shifting his position. His side produced a dull ache that seemed but a reflection of the searing pain that had accosted him when the bullet tore at his flesh last night. Last night? Had he escaped from jail less than twenty-four hours ago? An eternity seemed to have slipped by since Noah had been facing death.

"And then?" Angela asked, her right brow slightly raised.

"Then, the Lord called me to preach within a year. After helping me catch up on my academics, my father enrolled me in seminary and stood by me while I prepared for the ministry. I've been pastoring now for about eight years. About six months ago, I received a letter from a deacon, Miles Norman, in the First Congregational Church of Tyler, requesting that I come preach for them. At first, I declined." He shrugged. "I'm content with my congregation, and my parents have retired and are now members of my church. But when Mr. Norman continued to correspond, I eventually decided to visit them and prayerfully consider their invitation. Besides, I—my life lately seems to need a change." Noah stopped short of mentioning his deep desire for a wife. Instead, he examined the worn, patchwork quilt covering him.

"I consulted a fellow pastor—Dan Wilson—in Timpson. He encouraged me about the opportunity and even suggested that I could always move my parents with me. When they agreed to the possible opportunity, I decided to take the trip. Everything went fine at first. Then, when I pulled into Rusk, I decided to treat myself to a night's sleep in a real bed. When I placed my horse at the livery, the owner offered to rent me the spare room at the back of the stable. It was cheaper than a hotel, and I figured the Lord was smiling on me. But some time during the night, a couple of men broke into my room, gagged me, tied me up, and hauled me away."

Angela's eyes sparked with interest and alarm.

"They wore bandannas, and there was so little light I have no idea who they were. Oddly enough, they knew me, even called me by name. They threw me in front of the sheriff's office and knocked me out cold. When I woke up, it was close to dawn and the sheriff was standing over me. The next thing I knew, I was thrown in jail, tried for murder, and sentenced to hang."

"Someone is framing you," Angela muttered, her eyes wide.

A wave of fury washed upon Noah. "I know! Everyone who witnessed against me at the trial was convinced I was Rupert Denham and had killed their banker."

"Have you seen Denham's picture?" Angela asked.

"Yes. They shoved a wanted poster in my face the first chance they got."

"The two of you look almost exactly alike."

"I know. But I'm *not* Rupert Denham, and I have *never killed* another human being," Noah rushed. "Even during my prodigal years, I never stooped to murder."

"I believe you," Angela whispered, her tumultuous eyes seemingly tormented by her own admission.

Noah, breathless with her words, silently stared at Angela as a renewed sense of gratitude descended upon his soul. If Noah hadn't been injured, he would have twirled her around the room. "Thank God," he uttered.

Angela, tears burning her eyes, stood and walked toward one of the candles. She nervously toyed with the curved handle on the flat, tin holder and produced a sniffle.

The Bible verse that she had recently read became a recurring chant in her mind, *Trust in the Lord with all thine heart; and lean not unto thine own understanding. In all thy ways acknowledge him, and he shall direct thy paths.* This verse had sprang from the pages and branded itself upon Angela's spirit only minutes after her heavenward plea for help. The very first verse of that passage was "trust"—the one word that had been Angela's bane for over a decade. In three little words, *I believe you*, Angela had extended trust in Noah Thorndyke and his word. But she *did* believe him. Somehow, she saw Eric's horrible situation all over again in Noah Thorndyke. Furthermore, something in his dark eyes left no room for doubt— something that spoke of honor and righteousness and valor. Although Noah and Eric looked nothing alike, that same flame of honor now burning in Noah's eyes had once burned within the blue eyes of her brother.

Yet, despite what her heart whispered to her, Angela's extending the trust she had so long held at bay scared her beyond reason. As the tears silently trickled down her cheeks, she touched the candle's soft, warm wax, dripping down the taper's sides. And she knew without doubt that if Noah Thorndyke were not innocent that she was the biggest fool alive. Before that morning, she had never even seen this man. Now, she had placed her job and reputation on the line for him. The need to protect her own vulnerability left Angela pressing her lips together and whirling to face Noah.

"I do believe you, Mr. Thorndyke," she said. "But if I find out you're lying to me, I'll—I'll—"

He raised his brows.

"I'll turn you in faster than that bullet tore into your side. Do you understand me?" she asked, shaking her finger at his nose as if he were a truant school boy.

"Yes," he said solemnly. "But I can assure you that I *am* innocent, and I have *no idea* who Rupert Denham is."

"And, one other thing you need to understand," she continued as if he had never spoken. "I *will* help you get back on your feet and help all I can to get you back to your home, but that gives you no license to. . ." The memory of that intimate moment when his gaze trailed to her lips left her cheeks as warm as the candle wax clinging to her fingertips. Despite her own verbal spewing, Angela looked toward Noah's lips and wondered what she had been missing all these years. The heat in her cheeks rushed down her spine.

"Would you allow me to beg your humble forgiveness, Miss Isaacs," he said, his dark eyes spilling forth genuine repentance. "I have not been myself these past few hours. And well, if you must know. . ." Noah looked away and restlessly shifted, as if he were afraid of his own words. "I promise to behave as the consummate gentleman from henceforth during our association which, I hope, for your benefit, will remain brief," he said, his attention on the ladder.

Surprisingly, Angela felt none of the relief she had experienced throughout the years when one man or another attempted to court her and at last gave up. Instead, a tendril of disappointment sprouted deep within her heart.

"Thank you," she said dispassionately as she hurried toward the ladder. "The afternoon is waning and I have numerous chores to which I must tend. If you'll excuse me, please." Without looking back, Angela climbed the steep steps and began to close the cellar door.

But before the door settled into place, she heard Noah's soft words, like a warm spring breeze upon branches, left barren by winter's chill. "And what, fair lady, does your past hold?"

ð

Rupert Denham mumbled to himself and stroked his dark mustache. Impatiently, he grabbed for the scabbard at his side. With one deft move he whipped out a heavy knife and jabbed it in the tabletop. His thin-faced stepbrother, sitting across the dilapidated table, snatched his hand out of the way.

"Do that again, and you'll be sorry," Mark snarled.

"Well, he done ripped the bottom outa my plan!" Rupert shot back. "And you ain't done a thing to help."

Mark, eight years his brother's junior, wiped his face with a dirty sleeve and glared at his sibling. "What am I supposed to do but report what I learned? Would ya have me lyin' to ya?"

Denham, disgusted beyond reason, grabbed the knife's handle and maneuvered it in a slow circle until the tip loosened. He raised the knife and fiercely stabbed the table again. "No, but you could try killing Noah Thorndyke! I had him right where I wanted him and now you've lost him!"

As if he were searching for a weapon of his own, Mark glanced around the shabby, abandoned cabin that was nestled deep in the East Texas woods. "You got no right blamin' me," he growled. "If you want Thorndyke dead so bad, why didn't you go after him on your own?"

Denham glowered at his brother and knew he could produce no reply. Since the start of his mission to end Noah's life, Rupert had taken no chances on being identified. If and when Noah was dead, then Rupert would be dead—according to the law, anyway. And that meant freedom. Rupert scratched at his scraggly beard, grown in an attempt to disguise his appearance. That, plus the shoulder length, bushy hair made him look more like a bear than a man. However, until Noah was dead, Rupert was taking precious little risk of discovery.

With renewed frustration, Rupert sent a tin pan and fork sailing into the wall. The pottery mug, half full of cold coffee, tipped from the table, and landed in Mark's lap. "We got no food except some stinking beans and a piece of hog belly. I gotta come up with a new plan."

Standing, Mark Denham placed flattened hands on the graying table and lowered his face toward his elder brother. The afternoon sunshine, filtering through the milky windows, cast a glow upon his hard, gray eyes, making them seem more like granite. "You ain't gonna have me in them plans if you don't stop treatin' me like the dirt under your feet. I'm sick of it!" He grabbed a handful of Rupert's shirt. "I'm doing the best I can to help you and yer actin' like a bear! Now, you've got a choice, big brother," he sneered. "You can either stop yer stupidity or you can dig your way out of this one alone."

Rupert, shocked speechless, stared at his kid brother in disbelief. Never had Mark stood up to him so vehemently. And, for the first time, Rupert saw Mark as a man, not the kid he had helped raise. However, he could never let Mark get the upper hand. Standing, he jerked his brother's hand from his shirt and tightened his grip on his wrist. "Don't threaten me, *boy*," he growled. "If you leave me high and dry and I get caught, I'll tell every lawman who'll listen just how big of a help you've been in all our little projects. Understand?"

The edge in Mark's eyes dulled a bit, but the steel remained. "That ain't so, and you know it."

"Well, I've been lookin' for Noah ever since Pa told me about him on his deathbed! Now that I've found him, I'm not gonna let you ruin it for me! Pa might have spoiled you rotten, but I ain't yer pa! And I'll turn you in quick like if you back out on me."

The two embarked upon a silent contest of the wills, a contest Rupert won when his brother looked away.

"Go get us some firewood for tonight," Rupert snarled.

His mouth set in a rebellious line, Mark walked outside and slammed the door behind him.

Rupert ground his teeth together and kicked at the rickety chair he had just vacated. It toppled onto the grimy floor and seemed a symbol for his well-laid plan that had shattered at his feet. As bad as he hated to, he was going to have to involve Quincy in this deal. But Quincy never came cheap. The help of that crooked lawyer would probably cost Rupert every piece of the gold he and Mark had lifted from that bank in Rusk. However, the scheme would most likely insure Noah's death and Rupert's freedom. He could always replace the gold through another robbery. But his freedom was priceless.

"Mark!" he yelled. After striding toward the dilapidated door, he flung it open. "Mark! Come here! I want you to make a trip to town!"

seven

Saturday morning, Angela hitched her horse and buggy near Dogwood's General Store and cringed at the thought of having to make her way through the town, already bristling with the usual rush of Saturday traffic. Everywhere she turned, Angela saw farmers trading cattle; wives rushing here and there to stock up on provisions; children chasing and squealing along the boardwalks. Even though no one should suspect Angela was housing a supposed criminal, she felt as if her every expression announced the fact to the world.

She would not have come to town except that she did need a few supplies, and her patient had discreetly requested a bath. Angela, feeling as if she were taking a grave risk, had agreed to Noah's leaving the cellar while she was gone. After securely closing all curtains and shutters, Angela had left her metal tub full of warm water in the kitchen.

Fortunately, she had just finished sewing and mending some clothing for a man whose wife had died while giving birth to her tenth child. Since several of the family's children were her pupils, Angela had offered to assist the poor father in some of the housekeeping duties his wife had once performed. With a spirit of thankfulness, the struggling dad had given Angela three feed sacks full of torn clothing that needed mending—belonging to both him and the children. She had retrieved a pair of the man's overalls and a shirt for Noah to wear until she could wash his clothing.

With a deep breath, Angela screwed up every ounce of bravado she could muster and opened the store's door. The bell's cheery tingle greeted her as she stepped over the threshold. Instantly, the smells of coffee beans, peppermint, and leather assailed her. A number of customers milled around inspecting the various items, from horse harnesses to material for clothing to bags of cornmeal. Angela, keeping her face impassive, went to work gathering the sugar and coffee she needed. Next, she chose several spools of thread and a new package of needles then examined the light cotton, perfect for making fresh bandages. This morning, Mr. Thorndyke had moved more freely. She had even discovered him at dawn, standing near one of the cellar's narrow air vents, peering out for a limited view of the surrounding countryside.

At last, Angela had accumulated her supplies and stacked them by the cash register. The buxom Bess Tucker, the town busybody, stopped her usual round of gossip with one of the locals and made her way to the cash register, where she began ringing up Angela's bill. Jars of candy lined the wall behind the counter, and Angela recalled the awkward conversation she and Noah had exchanged last night when she delivered his supper. During their stilted words, he had mentioned loving licorice since he was a child. Perhaps the reason for their trivial conversation had been the increasing tension that seemed to simmer beneath the surface of their every encounter. If Mr. Thorndyke's liquid brown eyes were any indication, the man found Angela immeasurably pleasing. But now that Angela had decided he really was innocent, there was nothing left for them to discuss. *Nothing.* As she had promised, Angela would help him, and when he rode out of her life, she would dismiss him from her thoughts. For despite Angela's step of faith in believing his story, she would never trust her heart to another man. *Never.* The light of resignation in Noah's eyes suggested that he saw and understood more than Angela had ever stated.

"And will that be all?" Bess asked absently. Distracted by the increasing crowd, the fiery redhead gazed around the store.

"Um. . .add two cents worth of licorice to my order, please," Angela said as nonchalantly as she dared.

Bess looked at her quizzically. "Why Miss Isaacs, I thought you deplored licorice," she said, her brassy voice rising above the hum of the patrons. "Acquiring a new taste?"

A lull in the customers' various conversations made Angela feel as if all attention focused on her. Feigning an air of assurance, she chose to ignore Bess's question and simply paid her bill. A discreet glance over her shoulder proved that no one was interested in whether she hated licorice or ate sixteen pieces a day. Nonetheless, Angela's heart pounded as if she were on trial.

And the realization of the magnitude of the risk she was taking hit her anew.

Bess stacked Angela's purchases in the crate she had brought with her. Scooping up the crate in her arms, Angela turned toward the front door, certain she could not leave the store soon enough. A tall, wiry man standing near a display of Stetson hats in the front window turned to face her. A man, who happened to be Constable Parker. With a kind smile, he opened the door and followed Angela onto the boardwalk.

Trembling with fear, Angela produced a composed nod and stepped toward her horse and buggy.

" 'Scuse me, Miss Isaacs," Parker said politely. "But may I have a word with you in my office?"

Feeling as if she were caught in the direct path of a Texas twister, Angela swallowed hard. *What could he want with me?* her mind raced. *He knows I'm housing a criminal! But he can't know! How could he know? He must want something else. But what?* "Of course, Constable Parker," she said, amazed at her own dignified air.

He relieved her of the crate and motioned for her to precede him down the covered boardwalk, toward his office. Dust kicked up by wagons and stock attested to the need of another autumn shower. Angela, thankful that today's temperatures were cooler than yesterday's, raised her skirts a couple of inches to protect the hem. Several children called her name and waved. Angela, emulating her usual firm yet amiable air, returned their greetings. However, every word she spoke seemed to hold an undercurrent of duplicity. No trip to town had ever made her feel more conspicuous. Stepping up on the opposite walk, she shook her dress, then allowed Constable Parker to open the door to his office—a shadowed, windowless room, whose stone walls assured a cooler temperature during Texas heat waves.

Once inside, the constable turned up the lantern and offered Angela a rather unstable armchair. "Sorry, ma'am," he said, dropping his hat on the corner of his desk. The county don't give us a lot for furnishin's."

"That's perfectly fine," she answered, primly lowering herself into the chair that wobbled with her weight. Yet all the while Angela's stomach knotted into an ever tighter wad of tension.

Parker shuffled through the disarray of papers on his desk and drew out an oversized poster. "Ever seen this feller?" he asked casually.

Her worst fears confirmed, Angela forced her stiff fingers to accept the rough, printed paper from the lawman. Her free hand clutched the chair's arm and she felt as if the constable were scrutinizing her every move. "Sheriff Garner asked me the same thing yesterday morning, Constable," Angela said evenly.

"So you already know what the man looks like?"

"Yes," Angela said, deciding the best course of action was to look the lawman square in the eyes. She had learned through the years of dealing with children that the ones who made eye contact were usually the ones with the least to be ashamed of.

"Reason I'm askin' is, the sheriff found his horse not

far from your place and a spot in your garden that looked like somebody might have spent the night there."

"That's what he told me yesterday morning," Angela said.

"Blast that man," Parker growled. "He told me they escorted the kids home but never once mentioned showin' you the wanted poster. Now I've done gone and wasted your time—"

"It's quite all right," Angela said with a kind smile, feeling as if she would swoon with relief. "You're just trying to do your job. The sheriff was probably so tired from riding all night that he failed to report all the details to you."

"Thanks for your understandin' spirit, ma'am." With an apologetic smile, Parker reached for the poster. "The man's a killer and I just want you ta be safe. The sheriff says he's a master at lyin' and is even trying to pass himself off as a minister."

"Oh?" Angela asked, her face growing cold.

"Sure thing. That horse he was on wound up bein' Denham's. At first, the sheriff thought he had stole it, but come to find out, it was his own. Anyway, he told the sheriff from the start that he wasn't Rupert Denham, but a preacher man from Louisiana by the name of Noah Thorndyke. Sheriff says the criminal had tried to get them to look in his saddle bags but both the sheriff and the town was so convinced he had to be Denham that he didn't see no sense in it."

"Yes?"

"Well, we decided it might be best to go through them saddle bags and discovered some letters from a First Congregational Church in Tyler, Texas, addressed to a Reverend Noah Thorndyke, for sure."

Angela's attention remained riveted upon the graying constable as he stroked his wide sideburns and placed an elbow on the desk.

"But the best the sheriff and I can figure, there ain't no such church there. The sheriff's folks lives in Tyler, and there just ain't no such church."

Angela's hands shook as if *she* were the one accused of murder. She tightly wrapped her fingers around the velvet reticule lying in her lap, all the while praying that the constable did not notice her rapid pulse pounding against the base of her neck.

"And along with them letters and a mighty fine gold watch with the name 'Denham' engraved on the back, there was one of them wanted posters, all crumpled down in the bottom of the bag. So, the sheriff and I have done put it all together and decided the killer is tryin' to use them letters to somehow prove he's a preacher."

"Really?" Angela rasped, her mind spinning with questions: *Why was Noah carrying a wanted poster? He claimed he knew nothing about Rupert Denham before entering Rusk. And while the letters match his story, there's no such church. What does that mean other than he made up the whole story? His being in possession of that poster and watch suggests that he is Rupert Denham! Have I been duped? Have I allowed my brother's tragic story to blind me to the truth?*

Thoughts of Jason Wiley stomped through Angela's mind and she felt as though every breath had been snatched from her. The licorice residing in the crate on the constable's desk at once became symbolic of a long, ebony serpent, bent on poisoning Angela's life; a serpent, dwelling in the heart of the man who had tried his best to trick Angela; a man her heart had secretly wanted to please with the licorice, despite her mind's resolution to keep him at arm's length.

She opened her mouth, ready to blurt the exact location of Rupert Denham, but a flash of anxiety assaulted her spirit, and that Bible verse from the day before swept, once again, through her mind. *Trust in the Lord with all thine heart; and lean not unto thine own understanding. In all thy ways acknowledge him, and he shall direct thy paths.* Upon the heels of that verse came another disturbing thought. *Perhaps you should pray about this decision. . .pray, as you haven't prayed in years.*

"Well," the constable continued, "I guess I've taken enough of your time. Just keep your eyes open the next couple of days, Miss Isaacs. You're a woman alone out in them parts, and I don't want no harm to come to ye," he said with an assuring nod.

"And what of my students?" Angela asked, her voice sounding strained, even to her own ears. "Should we continue with school on Monday?" The question seemed insane, considering she was housing the supposed criminal, but Angela knew it was one she should ask.

"Might not hurt to wait till mid-week," Parker replied, pushing back his chair. "Have the preacher to announce in tomorrow's service that I asked you to hold off. By Wednesday, I look for that criminal to be out of Cherokee County—if he's as smart as he looks so far. Accordin' to the sheriff, Denham's injured but he ain't injured too bad or he'd have never given us the slip so soundly."

Angela stood on shaking legs. Never had she been so torn concerning what to do. Just about the time she had embraced Noah's innocence as fact, she was slapped with another round of incriminating evidence. Without a doubt, she did need to pray. Pray as she hadn't prayed in years.

"Thank you for your time, ma'am," Parker said, standing. "Can I get the crate for you? I hate that I done hauled you off up the street so far from yer buggy."

"No. That's fine," Angela rushed, reaching for the crate. "I can manage it. I'm sure—I'm sure you have many more pressing tasks."

As if to punctuate her remark, the office door banged open and a harassed-looking man entered. "There's a fight in front of the saloon," he barked out, and the constable dashed out the door before Angela had time to even gather her wits enough to walk.

Within minutes, she sprinted up the boardwalk and to her buggy. Angela deposited the crate behind the driver's bench. Placing one hand atop her conversation hat, decorated in plumes the color of evergreens, she embarked the buggy and gave the bay mare a gentle slap with the reins. The dependable creature trotted up the busy street and away from Dogwood.

Angela, burdened with the weight of the constable's news, held herself erect, her emotions in check, her mind in firm control. For if she allowed herself to slip in one area, she knew she would lose control in all areas. Although she left Dogwood's teaming streets behind, Angela felt as though the whole town still watched her, still speculating, still suspicious. And she *would not* give them reason to imagine that the conversation with Parker had in any way upset her.

Fifteen minutes into her journey, Angela's emotions would no longer remain in check. As the sight of a thick grove of pines came into view, she was reminded of a similar grove near her parents' homestead several miles south of Dogwood. A grove such as this had been her special sanctuary and haven of prayer during her younger years—a place where she met the Lord and He directed her path. It was among fragrant evergreens such as these that she learned to turn her heart toward her heavenly Father and seek His ways.

Her soul heaved within like a tumultuous sea, tormented by the breath of a livid hurricane. And Angela pulled the small carriage to a stop, allowing the reins to inch from her fingers. Her hands quivering, she covered her face and welcomed the pent-up tears. Tears of panic. Tears of tension. Tears of repentance.

"Oh Father," she said over a sob. "I don't know what—what to do. Please. . .please forgive me for—for waiting until such a dark m–moment to turn to You.

But—but I so desperately need your wisdom." She tried to catch her breath but only produced a strained hiccough. "Please direct my path, and—and show me—me whether I should turn in Noah or continue to help him. If he *really is* Rupert Denham. . ."

The repetitive, soft cooing of a dove on a distant, piney hill penetrated Angela's agitation and gradually wove an aura of peace around her spirit. After almost half an hour of quiet reflection amidst the lush countryside touched in gold, Angela understood that, for whatever reason, the Lord did not want her to report Noah's location to the authorities. A gentle assurance deep in her soul confirmed that Angela had been right in not blurting all to Constable Parker.

However, the confusion still remained over why Noah had been in possession of a wanted poster and a gold watch with "Denham" on the back. As Angela picked up the reins and began her journey anew, she purposed to tell Noah what Constable Parker had shared with her. Both the wanted poster and watch incriminated Noah and made him look as if he had lied to her. But Angela felt that the Lord was urging her to at least give him a chance to explain.

For the first time in over a decade, Angela Isaacs had begun the journey of allowing God to direct her path, of setting aside her own understanding, of trusting Him, even in the face of opposing logic.

But will you allow Me to heal your hurts? The thought pierced through her soul like a pinpoint of light, penetrating a pit as black as night. Angela recoiled from the notion. She had clung to the shadows of her painful past for so many years that they had become a symbol of security. As long as she hid behind the shadows, she took no risks with her heart. Releasing her heartache to God would result in His breaking down the wall that separated Angela from the rest of the world, a wall that prohibited her from developing intimacy in any new relationships—especially with the opposite sex.

Angela thought of Noah Thorndyke, of how he obviously admired her, of how she had enjoyed the presence of a man in her home, of how poignant her lonely existence now seemed. But the idea of releasing her past, even for someone like Noah, left Angela emotionally terrified.

❧

Deep in the east Texas woods, Rupert stood waiting beside the cabin's milky window. At long last, two horsemen approached through the thick, brushy woods. Rupert had waited all morning for their appearance.

Yesterday evening, he had sent Mark into Jacksonville, the town between Rusk and Dogwood, with the purpose of making Quincy Brown an offer. Hopefully, Quincy's accompanying Mark meant that the crooked lawyer had gleaned the information Rupert so desperately needed.

With jittery fingers, Rupert scratched at his beard. He would never let on, but Quincy made him nervous. While the lawyer and Rupert both made a profession of separating people from their money, Quincy knew how to do it legally. His sly use of the law left Rupert feeling at a disadvantage. The outlaw suspected that during one or two of their dealings Quincy had dealt him a raw deal. But Rupert had no choice in using him this time.

He settled onto the musty cot against the wall, feigning an attitude of nonchalance. But inside, he was wound tighter than a coiled watch spring. He reflected upon the last year. . .upon his learning from his dying father that he had a twin brother. . .upon his tracking down Noah in Mansfield, Louisiana, only to discover he was a stinkin' preacher. That within itself made destroying Noah all the more rewarding. For some evil serpent deep within Rupert hated the very thought of God and religion. He chuckled to himself as he recalled his scheme of enticing Noah to Texas—through fictitious letters from a fictitious church in Tyler looking to fill a fictitious pastoral position.

The door slowly creaked open, and Mark entered with Quincy on his heels. The erect and "dignified" lawyer discreetly practiced his deceit with anyone willing to produce his exorbitant fees. While many prominent citizens in the county paid respectful homage to Quincy, Rupert and his kind understood that the lawyer valued one thing above all others. Money. And lots of it. Quincy would stoop to any fraud, treachery, or cruelty for another dollar to bolster his burgeoning fortune.

The physical contrast between Mark and Quincy belied the similarities of their intents. While both were tall and lean, Mark looked the part of the typical dark-headed, buzzard-eyed, unshaven outlaw. Quincy, on the other hand, appeared as if he should be sitting in a tea parlor among the most dignified of society. The lawyer's freshly shaven face and long-tailed suit made Rupert want to gag. Only his keen, green eyes suggested he had the heart of a cobra.

"What do you need?" Quincy asked, peering at Rupert with an air of distaste.

"I'm in the middle of a killin'," Rupert drawled, never bothering to move from his reclining position. "Or haven't you already figured that one out?"

Quincy Brown's blond brow rose in surprise.

"What did you expect me to be needin' you for," Rupert growled, "to invite you to a ladies' quiltin'?"

"Mark only said you wanted any clues to where the law thought you were hiding."

Rupert produced a harsh laugh. "That's exactly what I wanted!"

Brown, his eyes narrowed, studied Rupert. "From what I gather, there was a rope awaiting you in Rusk and you sprang jail," he said in precise English.

"Think again," Rupert's voice taunted. The blond lawyer's jaw clenched, and Rupert knew his flippant air was having the annoying effect he desired. "Wasn't me in that jail cell. 'Twas my twin brother," he said with a satisfied smirk.

The astonishment in Quincy's eyes was almost worth every ounce of trouble this whole ordeal had cost Rupert. In all their dealings, the outlaw had never felt as if he possessed the upper hand with Quincy. The surge of power left him almost giddy with triumph. He casually stood and eyed Mark, who stirred the coals in the rock fireplace then laid a couple logs atop the red embers.

Quincy, crossing his arms, scrutinized Rupert. "Are you going to give me the details of this scheme or not?" His question held the nuance of a command.

Purposefully pausing, Rupert walked to the empty coffeepot and handed it to his younger brother. "Make some more," he said. Noting the flair of resentment in his brother eyes, Rupert decided Mark was long overdue a beating.

"My plan," Rupert said, straddling the rickety, wooden dining chair and dropping into it, "is to get my twin brother hanged so I can go free. The whole plan was workin' like a charm 'til that rat broke outa jail."

"I didn't even know you had a twin," Quincy said as Mark left the cabin in quest of some well water.

"Neither did I 'til 'bout a year ago. My pa told me all about him the day 'fore he died. My ma died when we was just babies. I was the healthy one of the two. Seems Noah couldn't stay well, and Pa was sure he was gonna die if he didn't get some medical care, but he didn't have no means to do that. So when he was passing through Mansfield, Louisiana, he left Noah on the porch of the local parson, named Thorndyke. My pa was the decent sort." Rupert produced a calculating smile. "The day 'fore he died, Pa told me I had a twin. He seemed to think that with him and Mark's ma both gone, Mark and me would like to know about another relative. But I had a better idea for my twin brother."

Mark entered, carrying the gray, rusted coffeepot full of water.

"I figured if I could somehow lure him into East Texas, I could get him arrested and hanged as me." Rupert observed Mark, dumping enough coffee into the pot for sixteen cups. "Not so much," he demanded. "It'll be so stiff we can't stomach it."

Clenching his jaw, Mark glowered at his brother. Without a word, he dropped the pot and the coffee bag on the table then stomped outside.

"Looks like your biggest fan is ready to brawl." Quincy pulled a long, thin cigar from his sorrel coat's inside pocket, smirking as if he relished the tension between the Denham brothers. The lawyer placed the cigar between even, white teeth and leaned toward the lantern, which gleamed from the table's center. He removed the sooty globe and inserted the tip of the cigar into the flame, puffing it until the end glowed and the room smelled of acrid smoke.

"He ain't nothin' but an overgrown boy," Denham said. "And he's long overdue a beatin'."

"That would be something to see," Quincy said, his eyes narrowing as he sucked a long draw on the cigar.

"Meaning?"

"He's as big as you are. Or haven't you noticed?"

"I didn't ask you to come out here to tell me what ya think of me and my brother," Rupert said evenly. "I want to know what you found out about where I'm s'posed to be hidin'."

"Oh, I found out a thing or two," Quincy said, brushing at his impeccable coat sleeve.

"And?" Denham asked, abruptly standing.

Quincy Brown stiffened as though ready to draw his sidearm at any given moment. Rupert hid his smile. He liked knowing Brown was on edge. Feigning nonchalance, Denham grabbed the warped, metal poker and stabbed at the crackling logs, all the while keeping his eye on the lawyer.

"I'll tell you everything I know as soon as you tell me where the gold is hidden. That was the deal Mark offered."

"Okay," Rupert said. "You'll find it 'bout fifty yards behind this cabin, under a big rock. As soon as you give me the information, you're free to go get it." The outlaw glanced out the cloudy window. "Hope you brought your big saddlebag."

"I came sufficiently prepared," Brown snapped.

"Great," Rupert said, chuckling to himself. Neither Quincy nor Mark knew that Rupert had dug up that gold last night and hid half of it in the cabin's attic. Quincy thought he was getting the whole cache. "Now what did you find out?"

"After Mark arrived, I wired a note to my contact— one of Sheriff Garner's deputies."

Rupert impatiently nodded.

"We agreed to meet last night, halfway between Jacksonville and Rusk. For a few pieces of gold, he told me that they found what they thought was your horse close to the schoolhouse just north of Dogwood, and they found signs of your spending the night in the school mistress's garden. There was blood smeared in the weeds as well as the outline of a man. The deputy said you took a bullet on your way out of town."

"But it warn't me," Rupert said, slowly tucking his soiled shirttail into his britches. Quincy noted the outlaw's every move. Just for meanness, Rupert picked up his pistol lying near the lantern and inserted it between his waist and his britches band.

"No," Quincy said, the cigar still firmly between his teeth.

"And what else?" Rupert asked, recalling the location of that particular schoolhouse, about fifteen or twenty minutes east of his present location. Denham had actually lifted a few heads of cattle not far from there the year before last.

"That's it. They think you've given them the slip."

Rupert, his mind whirling with possibilities, stared at the blazing logs. "And what about that schoolmarm? Ain't nobody questioned her 'bout whether or not she seen or helped a criminal?"

"Of course," Quincy said. "The deputy says she's not the kind to assist a criminal. She's the uptight, proper variety."

Squinting in calculation, Rupert held Quincy's snake-eyed gaze. "They think they're chasin' me, and they know I've given 'em the slip before, but I don't believe for one second a preacher-man would have enough weasel in him to put such a the slip on the law, especially if he was injured." Rupert paused as his mind began piecing together the mystery. "And you know somethin', without my beard and all this hair, I'm a good-lookin' devil—or so the ladies have told me."

Denham produced a lascivious grin. "I just wonder if maybe that schoolmarm might be more open to a man's company than she's lettin' on."

"I doubt it," Brown growled.

"Well, I aim to find out," Rupert replied. "I'm a wanted man, and I'll do anything to get my freedom— even if it means roughin' up a prude till she talks."

eight

Noah, enjoying his bath, soaked in the warm water as long as he dared. Finally, he got out, dried himself off, and was able to redress his wound, thankful that his side showed signs of healing. Nonetheless, Noah had barely donned the faded overalls and flannel shirt before exhaustion set in. He was certainly improving, but needed a few more days before he could travel. Already, Noah's thoughts were turning toward the possibilities of beginning his journey home under the cover of an inky night.

He stepped onto the ladder and descended the steps into the cellar. Welcoming the feel of the mattress beneath his back, Noah snuggled under the covers and closed his eyes. A sweet sensation of release washed over him as he dreamed of the woman of light and beauty who came to minister to him—his own angel. He relived the softness of her touch and the gentle manner in which she dressed his wound. He reached to touch her auburn hair only to have the breeze of his fantasy blow her away and bring with it a gray mist. . .

. . .A child's voice whimpered in the middle of the mist. Noah stepped forward. As he walked, the fog parted and the voice became more distinct. The vision of the previous dream swam before his eyes: an expansive, green lawn shaded by huge trees, the rock cottage, the oppressive mirror with its heavy baroque frame, and the little boy looking forlorn and lost. The child stood before the glass, his arms outstretched, and the mirror boy taunted him with grotesque facial expressions. A man of coarse appearance but loving countenance scolded the mirror boy for his behavior. He then regretfully looked at a gleaming, gold pocket watch, and turned beseeching eyes to Noah. With a glimmer of remorse in his eyes, he stepped from the mirror and picked up Noah, who had somehow become the toddler outside the mirror.

Feeling as if his heart were torn asunder, Noah clung to the rugged man whose face was moist with his own tears. A thick cough ravaged Noah's body and interrupted his tears. His eyes burned from fever. His head pounded as if someone were assaulting him with a hammer.

"No. . .no. . .no. . . ," he wailed in the voice of a child.

However, he was spun from the man's arms and plopped onto the banks of the Mississippi. Now, he was in his teen years, yet still his soul was crying, "No, no, no!"

Agitated, Noah struggled to sit up from the bank of the river, only to have someone pushing him back down into the warm, comfortable mud. He hollered out, struggling against his antagonist, only to feel a sharp tingle against his cheek. . .

. . .Noah's lids popped open, and he stared straight into a pair of beautiful brown eyes—the eyes of his angel. "M–Miss Isaacs?" he whispered, looking around the dirt cellar in confusion.

"I'm sorry," she said, and her eyes widened to emphasize her true remorse. "But I just slapped you."

"Yes." Noah gingerly touched his stinging cheek.

"I couldn't get you to wake up," she said, leaning away from him.

"What—what time is it?"

"It's supper time. I came down to tell you I have your tray prepared, but you were having a horrific nightmare. You were waving at the air, screaming 'No, Papa, no' at the top of your voice—but you sounded more like a young child than a man." She shuddered, and her expression reflected the very trauma that still left Noah's soul reeling with the devastation of pain. . .the pain of a child being abandoned by his father.

"Oh, no," Noah groaned, covering his face with trembling hands. All these years his past had seemed an enigma. Now, he felt as if the past were swallowing him alive. Never, until this very moment, had Noah linked his rebellious years on the river to the cry of his heart as a toddler.

Perhaps. . .just *perhaps* Noah had been searching for his father all those years on the Mississippi, searching for the teary-eyed man who had left his sick child upon the mercies of another family.

"Your dream—you were so—so disturbed," Angela said. "Are you okay?"

"It's the second time since yesterday I've had that dream," Noah said, staring blindly toward the ladder. "I keep dreaming about two boys. One is in a mirror; the other one is looking into the mirror. They're identical. But today—just now, I dreamed about a man with. . . with. . ." Noah strained to recall the details as he struggled to sit up. Quickly, Angela stuffed an extra pillow behind his shoulders. "The man was holding a gold watch. He kept looking at it, and—"

"A gold watch?" she asked, her face paling as if an apparition had sashayed between them.

"Yes—yes, a gold watch. He was crying. He stepped out of the mirror and picked up the little boy outside the mirror. But the boy was me now, and I was screaming, 'No, no, no.' " Then I landed on the banks of the Mississippi and you slapped me."

"Have you ever had these dreams before now?" Angela asked.

"No, never," Noah said, shaking his head in confusion.

"Do you think that the Lord is somehow trying to show you something?" Angela peered deeply into his eyes.

"As in?"

"Constable Parker asked me to come to his office today and showed me that wanted poster. He didn't know Sheriff Garner had already asked me about you."

"And what did you say?" Noah asked anxiously.

"I just told him that the sheriff had already asked me

if I had seen you, and the constable never pursued the subject."

Noah let out his pent-up breath, and Angela eyed him, a new hint of suspicion tugging at the corners of her lips. "But Parker did tell me that they went through your saddlebags and found a gold watch with the name 'Denham' engraved on the back."

Noah, astonished by her words, gripped the covers, and felt as if the gold watch from his dream was dangling before his eyes. "And I dreamed about a man with a gold watch," he rasped.

"Yes, and a mirror image of two boys."

He nodded.

"Have you ever contemplated the notion that you might have a twin brother, Mr. Thorndyke?" Angela swept aside of strand of hair from her eyes. The sagging bun atop her head had allowed numerous wisps to escape and fall in an attractive array around her face.

"A twin?" he whispered, feeling as if they were stumbling upon a definite possibility.

"It would make perfect sense. This Rupert Denham looks too much like you to be a mere look-alike."

"The boy in the mirror. . . ," Noah muttered, his heart pounding as if he were in the grips of the dream once more. "But how did that watch get into my saddlebag?" he asked, studying Angela's countenance, desperately searching for any sign that she might set aside her new suspicions and continue to believe in him. He saw the questions churning through her eyes; questions that suggested a gold watch in his saddlebag with "Denham" on the back would logically incriminate him.

"The constable said they also found the letters from the Tyler Congregational Church that you mentioned."

"Yes," Noah rushed. "I carried them with me as evidence that I was the man with whom they had been corresponding."

"Constable Parker says there is no First Congregational Church in Tyler. Sheriff Garner's folks live in Tyler. There's no such church, and. . .and. . ." She nervously licked her lips, "they also found one of those wanted posters with Rupert Denham's picture on it," she said softly, her gaze seeming to probe the very recesses of his heart.

His palms growing clammy, Noah shook his head in disbelief. "But how can it be? I never even *saw* that wanted poster until they shoved it in my face after locking me up, and I corresponded with that deacon—Miles Norman—for months."

"Do you think the whole thing was a setup?" Angela asked slowly, the momentary doubt in her eyes fluttering away.

The pieces of a puzzle seemed to be plopping into place one by one. "If I have a twin, and he's wanted for murder, and I'm killed in his place, then he goes free."

She nodded.

"Miles Norman probably doesn't even exist. And this Rupert Denham must have put the watch and the wanted poster in my saddlebags—just in case." Noah felt as if he were sinking into the grips of a muddy pit, bent on smothering the very life from him. "Rupert might very well have been the one who knocked me unconscious and dropped me outside the sheriff's office." A wave of terror washed upon the shores of Noah's soul. The truth at once became as clear as the waters of a chilling spring, bubbling from the side of a jagged mountain. "Dear Lord save me, could I have been framed by my own brother?"

"How do you feel?" Angela asked, standing. "Is there any way you could travel tonight?"

"Trying to get rid of me?" Noah asked with a teasing smile.

"I'm trying to arrange for your quick and efficient escape, Mr. Thorndyke," Angela said as if he were a hardheaded student. "If our theory is correct and this Rupert Denham is indeed after you, then he might very well be lurking in these woods, waiting on you to show yourself. The sooner you can get out of here, the better."

"I don't think I could make it very far tonight," Noah said. "That bath wore me out."

"Then we'll have to try for tomorrow night," Angela said practically. "Constable Parker asked me to announce in church tomorrow that there will be no school until Wednesday, in order to give you time to get far out of the area." Pausing, Angela produced a faint, although ironic, grin. "If I have to, I'll hide you under some quilts in the back of my buggy and try to get you as far south as possible before leaving you on your own with my extra horse. Of course, I would need to be back before dawn, so no one would suspect that I had been away." She turned for the ladder, her full, cotton skirt producing a delightful swish. "I'll be back with your supper."

Noah, deeply touched by her continued willingness to help him, could not help but ponder just how devoid his life had been of feminine intimacy. During all his interactions with this angel, just beneath the surface of his pressing thoughts of survival, Noah had wrestled with the possibility that God very well could be trying to answer his prayer for a mate in the personage of Miss Angela Isaacs. However, the two of them had only just met and the way things were progressing, Noah might very well escape in the night and never see her again. These facts left Noah feeling as if he were twirling in a whirlpool of distress, and he decided that he must— *absolutely must*—address the issue of their possible relationship. Who knew if he would have a better opportunity before his leaving tomorrow evening?

"Miss Isaacs," he said softly as she prepared to climb the ladder.

Raising her brows, she turned to face him, her expression still schooled into a firm mask that suggested a certain disinterest in Noah's plight. Yet, the stirrings of compassion and worry, churning through the velvety softness of her eyes, suggested that Miss Angela Isaacs was far more disturbed by his unfortunate circumstances than she was admitting.

"It's often during such an unusual state of affairs such as ours that people perhaps. . .breach. . .the norms of decorum. With this in mind, I would like to ask your forgiveness for what I am about to say. However, I feel that it must be said." Noah pushed aside the covers and moved his stiff body to the sitting position. While the bath had seemed to ease his aching side, now that he had lain dormant for several hours, the stiffness had reclaimed his right side with renewed vengeance. However, Noah persisted in standing, even in the face of Angela's protests. Noah simply would not address such monumental issues with a lady while he was on his back. He would not.

"As I was saying, Miss Isaacs," Noah continued, moving to the ladder to grip it for support. "Before I started this journey, I prayed that the Lord would somehow use my trip to introduce me to the woman He has chosen for me."

Her sudden intake of breath and astounded expression attested to Angela's full comprehension of Noah's intent. "Mr. Thorndyke, *please*," she gasped. "We only just met, and I certainly couldn't imagine that you would dare *suggest*—"

"I am suggesting nothing, madam," Noah said gravely, his stomach fluttering as if he were sixteen and courting his first belle. And just as he had yesterday when her watch chain entangled itself in his shirt's button, Noah's traitorous mind pined to feel her lips against his, longed to feel her warmth in the circle of his arms. "I am simply asking your p–permission. . ." His voice's telltale wobble revealed the uncontrollable shaking of his legs. "I am asking your permission for me to correspond with you in the coming months, should—should I be fortunate enough to escape this wretched situation and find refuge in my home." Despite his better judgment, Noah's gaze trailed to Angela's lips; lips the color of summer's first peaches; lips that were quivering as if he had just kissed her.

Noah dared to reach toward her cheek and stroke its softness. All vestiges of the controlled matron vanished, replaced by a vulnerable woman who now returned Noah's warm appraisal. "I must admit that I have found in you the most becoming woman I have yet to make the acquaintance of. The thought of my departing—without ever stating my thoughts—leaves me somewhat in a panic. I have lain here and planned the whole thing. I was thinking that I would adopt a pseudonym for purpose of our writing. That way, the law would never suspect we were writing to one another. I pray that you'll forgive my forward overtures, but, as I already said, the duress of our unusual circumstances leaves me no choice."

The moment, froth with expectation, extended an eternity, and Noah could only pray that Miss Isaacs would agree to his petition. However, instead of answering, she looked away, fidgeted, pressed her lips together, and dashed up the short ladder without so much as a backward glance.

"Miss Isaacs?" Noah called in alarm.

Her back rigid, Angela stopped near the top and never even glanced over her shoulder. "Mr. Thorndyke," she said, her voice vibrating with the tension of the moment, "I find your overtures highly inappropriate and shocking to the point of disbelief. I will assist you back to your home all that I possibly can, but *please*, do not mention your fantastical musings again." Without another word, she ascended the remaining space and prepared to step off the ladder.

And a veil of bafflement settled upon Noah's mind. "You are risking your reputation and job to help me, yet you are scandalized by my overtures?" his perplexed tones reflected his complete confusion.

Her back still to him, Angela halted once again. "My assisting you has nothing to do with any hopes on my part of romantic involvement," she said in condescending tones that suggested she was growing increasingly offended with each passing word. "I have prayed about this whole situation and feel that the Lord is directing me to assist you. That is all there is to it."

"So, you are as much a woman of God as I presumed you to be."

These words instigated her pivoting to face him. "I would love to tell you that you have presumed correctly," she said, a note of regret in her voice. "But I have spent many—many. . . ," she cleared her throat, ". . .many years not. . .um. . .your present situation has driven me to my knees in a way that I have refrained from in years."

Noah, surprised by her admission, raised his brows, and she looked away as if the disclosure brought her deep shame. As the seconds ticked by, Noah mused about what must have caused a woman who knew her Bible so well to distance herself from its Author. The vulnerable twist to her lips and her continued insistence to keep Noah at arms' length suggested a heart torn asunder. Yesterday, Noah had asked her about her past, never once expecting a reply. But today, the past he had inquired about became the inevitable deduction of a sharp mind. "Who was he, Angela?" Noah dared to say, hoping all the while his assumption was indeed the correct one. "Who was the one who broke your heart?"

With another faint gasp, Miss Isaacs clamored into the kitchen, knelt beside the cellar door, and peered down at Noah. Her eyes, sparkling with unshed tears, reminded him of gleaming, mahogany-colored stones under the surface of a mountainous brook. "First, I will have you remember, *Mr. Thorndyke*, that I have yet to give you permission to address me by my given name. Second, while your previous comments were fantastical, your present remarks are beyond reprehensible," the word squeaked out, attesting to her rising irritation, as did her delightfully flushed cheeks. "*Please*, keep your inappropriate remarks to *yourself!*" She rose and stomped away, leaving Noah feeling as if he had been verbally slapped.

So much for my schemes, he thought. His heart heavy, Noah slowly walked back toward the makeshift bed and lowered himself onto the mattress. Despite the strain of the current situation, the smells of the evening meal wafting through the cellar door left his stomach complaining about its empty status. Yet, his heart felt just as empty. At long last, he had met a woman who seemed to be a potential lifetime companion, and she was so wrapped up in her past that she was blind to the present.

ᨠ

Angela rushed to her bedroom, closed the door, and

collapsed onto her bed. Covering her face, she allowed the tears to flow while stifling any noises that would suggest she was crying. She relived the moment that Noah touched her face, a moment that brought back a wave of emotion she had not experienced in years. She dared to ponder the possibilities of love, of joining her life with a man of honor. Her traitorous mind filled with images of Noah—the warmth of his touch, the velvet softness of his eyes, the expectation in his voice when he asked if she would correspond with him. His words, so imploring, had charged her soul and fanned the flame of attraction which had begun a slow burn in that moment when her watch chain tangled in his button.

The potency of these emotions terrified Angela, terrified her beyond reason. Shivering, she buried her face into the homespun quilt that smelled of lye soap. Angela, paralyzed by anxiety, contemplated the potential for her heart to be broken again. And she knew that, despite her reaction to Mr. Thorndyke, she could never allow him to court her—either in person or by mail.

Yet, a psalm she memorized in childhood waltzed among her troubled thoughts to suggest a new manner of introspection. *I will lift up mine eyes unto the hills, from whence cometh my help. My help cometh from the Lord, which made heaven and earth.* As if drawn by a power greater than herself, Angela dried her eyes on the edge of the quilt and looked out her opened bedroom window, toward the surrounding East Texas hills. The sun's last rays illuminated the countryside, touched with a hint of autumn's gold. A dove, softly cooing, wove an aura of tranquillity upon the whole scenic view. The small schoolhouse that sat about a hundred yards away tugged at Angela's heart. That schoolhouse represented her whole life. She had never once hesitated to weave every fiber of her heart into the lives of her students. Her past pain, her horribly humiliating experience with Jason Wiley, had left her no choice but to isolate herself from romance, but Angela had never once isolated herself from interacting in the lives of her pupils.

But the love of a noble man would make life so much more fulfilling. The thought left Angela blinking, and on the heels of that thought came the psalm once again. *I will lift up mine eyes unto the hills, from whence cometh my help. My help cometh from the Lord, which made heaven and earth.*

I will heal your heart, if only you will lift your eyes to Me and let Me help you. The words swirled through her soul, sending a rush of tingles down her spine, and Angela knew that God was nudging her toward relinquishing her past. But the past was her shield, her protector, her whole identity. Newly terrified, Angela covered her face again and doubted that she even knew how to release her past.

nine

The next morning, Angela pulled her carriage into the country churchyard and noted the group of people standing in front of the white, one-room church. The numerous, tall windows and white steeple seemed as much a part of the fabric of Angela's life as did her parents' own farmhouse, south of Dogwood. The autumn morning's brisk breeze chilled the air even more than yesterday. Angela's nose tingled as that cold breeze, rustling the surrounding pines, scurried around her Sunday hat. However, that cold wind felt as if it blew from the very portals of Angela's soul.

This morning, as she had yesterday evening, Angela delivered Mr. Thorndyke his meal, along with a thick helping of stony silence. He never said a word, but Angela felt his ardent gaze upon her. Already, she anxiously awaited tonight when she would assist the man in leaving the premises. Even if she had to squeeze him behind the carriage's driver's bench, cover him with quilts, and drive all night long, Angela would do anything to remove his troubling presence from her home.

After her silent yet potent cry yesterday evening, Angela had hardened her heart all the more against the notion of God's helping her recover from her past pain. In short, the longer she thought of releasing her past, the more apprehensive she grew. Trying to focus on the task at hand proved a convenient means to escape her troubling thoughts. Angela pulled in among the eclectic array of buckboards, wagons, buggies, and the Griffin's carriage brought all the way from Dallas by a neighbor's well-to-do cousin.

She spotted Rachel and Travis, standing under a big sycamore talking to Travis's brother, Levi, and his wife, Magnolia. In her arms, Magnolia held their baby daughter. The blissful blush on her cheeks attested to her happiness with life. While Rachel cooed over Magnolia's baby, her redheaded toddler, fondly dubbed Little Trav, hung on Rachel's emerald-colored skirt and tried to play peek-a-boo with a disinterested squirrel. Angela would never stop marveling at God's providing an adopted child for Rachel and Travis immediately after they lost their firstborn. And Little Trav, with his red hair like Rachel's, and green eyes like Travis, looked as if God had designed him especially for them.

Rachel, recognizing her cousin's buggy, waved to Angela, scooped up Little Trav, and excused herself from the discussion. As Angela stepped down from her carriage, Rachel gripped her arm and smiled into her eyes as if she were searching Angela's expression for any traces of Friday's strained conversation.

Angela, determined to place her younger cousin at ease, returned Rachel's smile and tried to put forth as relaxed a manner as was humanly possible under the present circumstances.

"I'm so glad to see you," Rachel whispered with

excitement. "Travis worked half the night on his sermon and I think I'm as nervous as he is. Since this is his first time to preach, he needs our prayers."

"I forgot that Pastor Eakin asked him to fill the pulpit today," Angela said, reflecting that the distractions of her life since Friday had left her almost forgetting her own name. "Rumor has it he's out preaching at another church in lieu of a call. Have you heard?"

"Yes," Rachel said, pushing a strand of auburn hair away from her face. "That seems to be true. Brother Eakin told Travis when he asked him to fill the pulpit today that he feels the Lord is asking him to move to this new church—just outside Dallas. We all can't imagine what it's gonna be like without him, but the Lord will provide. Meanwhile, Travis is really nervous. He's already planning to head up a pulpit committee and find a preacher soon. I think he did enjoy preparing today's sermon, but the thought of having to fill in until we find a pastor. . . ." Rachel left the rest unsaid.

"It's hard to picture Travis being nervous," Angela continued with her usual assurance. "With his oratory skills from law school and knowledge of scriptures, I'm sure he'll do exceptionally well and would continue to do well long-term, if the need arose."

Rachel gently squeezed Angela's hand. "I wouldn't share this with anyone except you, but last night Travis prayed over the sermon 'til he almost cried. When we prayed together, he said he feels as if the Lord has given him a message for a specific person today."

"Travis is a wonderful man," Angela said absently,

her mind drawn to Noah. He too, seemed sincere and wonderful, and Angela prayed he wouldn't needlessly lose his life. She scanned the countryside, wondering if Rupert Denham might be lurking behind one of the myriad of trees, covering the rolling hills.

For the first time since her petulant verbal outpouring, Angela felt mean-spirited for her waspish response to Noah's humble request to correspond with her. Her resolved desire to see him gone wavered in the memory of her own rudeness. Angela extended her arms to Little Trav who gleefully fell into her embrace. With Rachel at her side, she turned toward the church. But the closer she walked to the house of God, the more she felt the Lord's gentle tug on her heart. For the last several years, Angela had attended church as a necessary duty, required by her teaching contract. But today's pending service already felt different—as if Angela were embarking upon a new spiritual journey. Even now, she sensed the Lord's holy scalpel applying pressure to the cancer of her emotional wounds, and Angela wondered if perhaps she were the one whom Travis's sermon would touch.

❧

Noah finished the breakfast that Angela had silently served him before her departure for church. His heart heavy, he gripped the mug of lukewarm coffee and stood to walk to the air vent of his cellar abode. Although his side was still stiff, Noah felt much better this morning, much better than he had felt even last night. He peered through the air vent and drank in his limited view of rolling, East Texas hills. In the distance, a rooster crowed, hens clucked, and a woodpecker hammered against a tree.

The plan that had begun to nibble at the corners of Noah's mind last night, before he fell asleep, now resurrected itself. Ever since Noah had dared to ask Angela about the possibilities of their corresponding, she had turned into nothing short of an ice maiden, ready to freeze his soul with her very presence. Without doubt, the woman was ready to be rid of Noah. And, if that were the case, perhaps Noah should grant her the wishes of her heart. He had assumed she would attend church this morning; his assumptions proved correct. All Noah needed to proceed with his plan was a bonnet, a house robe, and hopefully, a horse. Miss Isaacs had mentioned an extra horse when she spoke of assisting him in his getaway.

"Well, it looks like I'll save you the worry, my dear Miss Isaacs," Noah muttered irritably. He took a final swallow of the strong, black coffee and decided to enact his plan. All he needed to do was make a trip to Angela's bedroom and borrow the items of clothing and find a pen and ink along with paper. Noah would take her horse but assure her he would send the money to cover the purchase of a new one as well as provide for the missing clothing.

With his decision made, Noah set his coffee cup on the tray beside his mattress and swiveled to face the cellar ladder. Yet, a melancholy veil draped across his spirit, a veil that seemed as thick as the despondency

that had visited Noah after those wretched dreams. For
the first time in his life, Noah had tasted the despair of
being abandoned as a sickly child. However, experiencing
that pain had somehow breached a gap in Noah's soul,
a gap that had held a mystery. Likewise, Noah's tasting
the possibility of developing a relationship with a
delightful woman had left him longing to fill the gap-
ing hole in his life marked "wife and family"—the hole
he had pleaded with the Lord to fill. But Miss Isaacs
was not the least bit interested, or so she said. Noah
wasn't blind. He sensed that she found him alluring,
but that seemed to matter little to Miss Isaacs.

Pressing his lips together, Noah ascended the ladder
and pushed open the cellar door. If he left now and traveled north, he could cross over the Louisiana border,
hopefully by midnight, before heading south, toward his
home. As he stepped into the kitchen, his side caught,
and Noah winced against the sharp pain, shooting
toward his ribs. *Dear Lord*, he prayed. *You preserved my
life this far. Please go with me now.*

ば

Rupert and Mark hovered in the woods behind the
schoolhouse until the teacher's buggy disappeared up
the dusty, narrow road. Then, they traipsed through the
woods and neared the teacher's house.

Rupert, gripping the binoculars, sensed Mark's
resentment, growing out of proportion. However, Rupert
firmly maintained the upper hand, never once showing a
sign of weakness to the younger man.

They paused on the edge of the woods and Rupert

scanned the two-hundred-yard space between their location and Angela's house. Next, he glanced across the countryside one more time, just to ease his quivering nerves. No other houses were in sight and the countryside appeared uninhabited as far as the eye could see. He and Mark had specifically planned to begin the hunt for Noah on Sunday morning, when the teacher would hopefully leave for church. If they didn't find Noah at the teacher's they planned to methodically break into every house in the vicinity until they found him. By starting with the teacher, they were simply playing a hunch and following the lead that Quincy had given them.

"Okay, here's the plan," Rupert whispered. "We run to the back door and pry it open with that poker you're carrying. I want us in and out as quick as possible. If we don't find no signs of him then we go to the schoolhouse and make sure he ain't there. From here, we'll go north and hit the next house we come to—if 'n they're at church too. Got it?"

"I got it back at the cabin," Mark said, his mouth in a sullen line.

Rupert, his patience wearing thin, grabbed a handful of Mark's smudged shirt and yanked him close. "Listen, *you*, I don't know what bur you've got under your saddle lately, but it's time to straighten up," he growled, his gut tight with irritation.

Mark squinted, and his right eye twitched. Clenching his teeth, he deliberately pried Rupert's hand from his shirt. "I know you didn't give Quincy all that gold," he sneered. "I saw him dig it up, and it was only half what you got from the bank."

"What are ya gettin' at?" Rupert said, surprised by Mark's power of observation.

"I *mean*. . .you're trying to make me believe you ain't got it." A rooster crowed from near the outhouse as if to punctuate Mark's claim. "And I don't think it's the first time, either."

"I'll wind up payin' for yer upkeep anyway," Rupert said.

"I'm tired of you payin' for my upkeep. I'm a grown man. I ain't no stinkin' kid anymore, and I deserve—"

"Shut up about what you *deserve*," Rupert snarled as a cool breeze scampered across the branches, decorated in gold-touched leaves. "From the time Paw first took sick ten years ago up 'til today, I've taken you under wing. Now you act like I owe you somethin'."

"Well, I—"

"Shut up," Rupert snapped. "Just shut up and let's do what we came to do. After this is all over, if you want to be on yer own so bad, then I'll give you half of what's left of that gold and you can hit the trail. You're gettin' to be more trouble than yer worth." Rupert fingered his pistol, safely tucked in his holster, and hoped he didn't have to pull it on Mark. He wouldn't shoot the boy out of anything but self-defense. But presently, the resentment in Mark's eyes bordered on hate, and Rupert no longer trusted him. Once they found Noah and saw him safely hanged, Rupert would be glad for Mark to set out on his own.

He prepared to step from the edge of the woods and motioned for his brother to follow. However, a woman, dressed in a bonnet and a frilly dress of sorts, walked out of the back door and toward the small barn, north of the teacher's house. But the longer Rupert watched that woman, the more he noticed that she really walked like a man.

❧

Angela held Little Trav close and followed Rachel up the few steps leading to the church door. While Rachel continued a light-hearted banter, Angela held the baby close and playfully intercepted his chubby hand as he reached for her plumed conversation hat. His green eyes sparkled merrily as he charmingly tried to say "hat" but much of the toddler's allure was lost on Angela.

Instead, yesterday's prayer time, among that grove of pines, invaded Angela's thoughts. She had leaned upon the guidance of the Lord to determine Noah's fate. Now, for the first time since her heated rejection of Noah's romantic overtures, Angela wondered if she should dare ask the Lord to guide her decision about Mr. Thorndyke's correspondence. She had never once prayed about God's will in her interacting with Noah.

"Is that all right with you?" Rachel asked, turning at the door to face Angela, her brown eyes alight with the reflection of a woman in love with life, with her husband, her child, and her Lord.

"What?" Angela asked.

Before Rachel repeated her question, she eyed Angela,

a cloak of apprehension settling upon her features. "You seem so distracted," she said softly. "Just like Friday. This is not like you. Are you sure you're all right, Angel? There's just—just something—some shadow in your eyes that—that—it's almost scary—almost as if Dr. Engle has given you a horrible diagnosis or something."

Angela swallowed hard and wondered why she ever thought she could hide anything from Rachel. Even though Angela was a full decade older than her cousin, Rachel possessed a spirit of discernment that increased as she matured. "I'm sorry," Angela said. "There's a lot on my mind. What was your question?"

Her heart pounding, she contemplated telling Travis and Rachel about Mr. Thorndyke's predicament. Travis would assuredly be better equipped to assist Noah out of the state than would Angela. She considered afresh the impact such an escapade might have on her teaching position. Were Angela discovered out alone during the night, her actions would be viewed as outrageous. Indeed, the whole countryside would be aflame with gossip before sunset. Furthermore, if anyone found out that a man was involved, Angela would be dismissed from her teaching post immediately. In order to minimize the chances of anyone discovering her nocturnal journey, she would be forced to be back home before dawn. However, Travis could travel all night and spend most of the day tomorrow getting back home. Given Travis's duties at the ranch, he had ample reasons to be gone overnight.

A group of church members ambled up the steps, and

Angela followed Rachel into the quaint, country church.
The hardwood floors gleamed in the morning's light,
spilling through the windows that each spanned five feet
tall. The polished pews were already filling with church
members and Rachel scanned the last few pews. "When
we were outside, I was just asking if you would mind sitting on the back pew with me," Rachel said. "Travis will
need to sit up front, and Little Trav has a way of distracting everyone if I sit up there."

"Of course, I'll sit with you," Angela said as Little
Trav squirmed in her arms. His blue striped jacket,
made of wool, had suddenly become too confining for
him and he tugged at the sleeves as if he were a caged
animal.

"Here, let me have him," Rachel said, reaching for
her son. "He's so hot-natured." Immediately, the young
mother found a spot on the last pew and began tending
her baby.

Angela settled on the hard pew beside her cousin and
something in the pit of her stomach twisted as she
observed the unbreakable bond between mother and
child. Fleetingly, she wondered what it would be like to
have her own child. Over the years, Angela had chan-
neled all maternal instincts toward her students, but a
new longing swept over her, a longing to have a family
of her own. Yet, that longing could only be fulfilled if
she were willing to take another chance on love. *All
Noah Thorndyke asked was permission to correspond.
What is that going to hurt?* she thought. Angela's lips
trembled with indecision. Her eyes stung, and an unex-

pected tear trickled from the corner. Shamefully, she dashed aside the tear, hoping no one noticed her display of seemingly irrational emotions.

However, Rachel noticed. She once again observed Angela, a grave look of concern spilling from her countenance, a look that said, *Please tell me what is wrong. I'll help you all I can.*

But the service began, the music started, and Angela mechanically mouthed the first stanza of the opening hymn. The voice of the organ exploded in her ears like the crashing of trees in a landslide. Songs, prayers, and announcements marched in succession while visions of Noah, forlornly locked away in the cellar, played upon Angela's mind. *All Noah asked was permission to correspond*, she thought again and again and again, while reliving her harsh treatment toward him. Slowly, a veil of anxiety cloaked itself around Angela's soul and left her debating her quick and definite "no" to Noah's overtures. Furthermore, the Lord seemed to whisper to her soul that this should be a matter of prayer. She had trusted God's guidance concerning Noah's innocence; perhaps the time had come to begin the journey from behind the shadows of her past and into the sunshine of the present and future. Yet with these very musings, Angela's heart constricted in alarm.

Finally, Travis Campbell stood and the entire congregation, including Little Trav, focused solely on the tall rancher. He approached the well-used pulpit and awkwardly rustled the pages of his worn Bible until he found the proper page. His fingers moved to the designated spot in the text.

"Da Da!" Little Trav exclaimed and the whole congregation produced a group chuckle.

Rachel, her cheeks reddening, tried to cover the baby's mouth, but he wiggled out of her reach and hollered all the louder, "Da Da, Da Da, *Da Da!*"

More laughter rose from the group, and Angela couldn't contain the bubble of joy mounting in her soul.

Travis, his eyes glowing with love, gazed toward his wife and child. "At least I have one fan in the crowd," he said, and the congregation burst into a round of applause, mixed with new guffaws.

"Excuse me," Rachel whispered, her expression a mixture of motherly exasperation and humored adoration. "But I'm going to have to take him out." She rose, and Angela moved her legs to the side so her cousin could exit. Once Rachel passed, Angela arranged her skirts and prepared to open her Bible.

Upon the heels of Rachel's departure and Little Trav's persistent calls, the congregation turned its sole focus to Travis and he cleared his throat. "I'll be reading two passages today. The first one is found in Proverbs 3:5–6. Angela compulsively gripped her Bible without ever opening it. She gazed at the top of the pew in front of her and held her breath as Travis read the words, so fresh in her memory. "Trust in the Lord with all thine heart; and lean not unto thine own understanding. In all thy ways acknowledge him, and he shall direct thy paths."

Travis paused and glanced over the congregation as if he were searching for the one person whom these scriptures would touch. "The other passage that the Lord has laid upon my heart is Psalm 121." He looked downward and began reading once more. "I will lift up mine eyes unto the hills, from whence cometh my help. My help cometh from the Lord, which made heaven and earth. . ."

Immediately, Angela felt as if the whole church were empty. . .empty of everyone but her and the Lord and a mellow voice, reading a Divine message, especially for her. Her eyes pooled in tears as wave upon wave of God's love rushed into the caverns of her hollow soul.

"He will not suffer thy foot to be moved," Travis continued, "he that keepeth thee will not slumber. Behold, he that keepeth Israel shall neither slumber nor sleep. The Lord is thy keeper: the Lord is thy shade upon thy right hand. The sun shall not smite thee by day, nor the moon by night. The Lord shall preserve thee from all evil: he shall preserve thy soul. The Lord shall preserve thy going out and thy coming in from this time forth, and even for evermore."

As Travis began expounding on the verses, Angela's heart poured out a cry to her Holy Creator. *Oh Lord*, she pleaded, the Bible trembling as if it were an extension of her own hands. *I desperately need You to help me, and to—to preserve my soul. Show me how to acknowledge you in all my ways—even when it comes to the possibilities of courtship. I'm so out of practice in acknowledging You. I'm not even sure if I know how. And then there are these shadows from the past, from—from what Jason Wiley did to me. Oh Lord, show me how to let them go.*

ten

Peering at the lone, ebony horse residing in the north pasture, Noah continued his swift trek toward the tiny, shabby barn. Even though there was no sight of anyone in the area, he felt as if every eye in the county were upon him. Despite the cool temperatures, Noah perspired from anxiety alone. He dashed aside the thin film of sweat that was forming where the bonnet met the sides of his face. A walk that took only two minutes felt as if it spanned two hours.

At last, Noah stepped into the shadowed barn that smelled of horse oats and straw and allowed his eyes to adjust to the difference in light. The barn was equipped with the usual garden tools, a few bails of hay, and even several small crates that appeared to hold various teaching tools as well as material. Two stalls took up most of the far wall. On one of those stalls hung a saddle. Noah trudged toward the saddle, the pain in his side gradually increasing with his every move.

Perhaps this idea wasn't such a good one, he thought as he strained to pull the saddle from its position. A large part of his desire to leave stemmed from embarrassment and injured pride laced with exasperation over Miss Isaacs' rejection of his overtures. Momentarily, Noah hesitated and wondered if his leaving in such fashion was either gracious or polite. *But on the other hand,* he reasoned with himself, *she acts as if she will be thrilled when I do leave. And my leaving is inevitable.*

Once more he saw the merciless eyes of the jury and heard the cries of excitement in the packed courtroom when they read the verdict. *Guilty!* The word had seemed to squeeze the very breath out of Noah, as if the noose were already tightening around his neck. *If they catch me again, they will undoubtedly hang me on the spot.* That fact alone spurred him forward. Gritting his teeth against the dull ache in his side, Noah hoisted the saddle onto his shoulder and trudged toward the barn door, all the while praying that the Lord would protect him until he safely arrived home. But just as Noah stepped out of the barn, a sharp blow met the back of his skull. Shocked, he cried out in pain, then everything went black.

&

After church, Angela wasted little time driving her carriage the brief distance back to her cottage. She stopped her dappled gray mare near the aging barn and made short work of releasing the horse from her harness and leading her into the pasture, where she was greeted by the ebony stallion. Angela had bought the stallion only two months before as an investment. She hoped the two horses would soon produce a colt that she could possibly sell for a profit.

Within minutes, Angela laid the heavy harness and accompanying paraphernalia in the barn. On the way out, she noticed one of her yellow summer bonnets, lying crumpled, just inside the door. Perplexed, she picked up the bonnet. Angela thought she remembered pushing aside the bonnet that morning when she reached for her felt church hat, the color of cedars.

Gripping the bonnet, Angela chose not to puzzle over the diminutive mystery. Instead, she focused on the task ahead of her, a task that left her palms sweaty and her heart racing. There were several items of business she needed to address with Mr. Thorndyke. First, Angela felt that the Lord was showing her she owed the gentleman an apology and an explanation for her rude behavior.

Travis's soft, yet potent sermon had affected Angela on numerous levels. Although she still wasn't certain she was indeed ready for any romantic involvement, Angela had decided to tell Mr. Thorndyke that he was welcome to write her, once he arrived safely home. The prospect left her both giddy with anticipation and timorous beyond expression. However, the same thought that had begun a chant during that church service once more became her companion: *I'm not agreeing to marry him. What harm can come from corresponding with the man? If I feel too terribly uncomfortable, I will just tell him to stop writing.*

Along with the issues of their correspondence, Angela also needed to discuss Mr. Thorndyke's pending escape that very night. She wanted to ask his permission to request Travis's assistance. When she fervently shared with Travis just how much she enjoyed his sermon, Angela had been tempted to take him aside and request his services then, but she had stayed her request. Angela did not want to make her final decision before discussing the possibility with Noah. She hoped Travis would take her and Noah's word concerning his innocence, but there was a certain risk that Travis would not believe Noah's story.

Still gripping the yellow bonnet, Angela opened her back door and allowed Grey to slip in ahead of her. The house cat meowed pitifully, as if she hadn't eaten in weeks. Smiling in her direction, Angela said, "I'll get you another bowl of milk in just a—" Angela stopped. The cellar door gaped open, and she wondered why Mr. Thorndyke would open the door in her absence.

"Mr. Thorndyke?" she softly called into the dark cellar. When silence greeted her, Angela said his name again. A nauseous knot formed in the pit of her tightened stomach, and she gazed toward her small parlor in hopes of catching sight of her patient there. Her heart wildly pounding, Angela dropped her reticule and the bonnet on the kitchen table. That's when she saw the edge of a note, peeking from beneath the straw mat where she took her meals. Only the words *Miss Angela Isaacs* were visible on the beige paper.

Her hands trembling, Angela pulled the paper from under the mat and glanced at the signature at the bottom to see the words, *Admirably yours, Rev. Noah Thorndyke* scrawled beneath several lines of script. Her eyes misting, Angela sank into the nearby kitchen chair and swallowed against the lump in her throat. Dreading what the note might say, she closed her eyes and took several steadying breaths. At last, Angela forced herself to focus on the letter.

Dear Miss Isaacs,

Please allow me to beg your forgiveness for intruding upon your privacy the last few days. However, I must admit that you were an answer to my prayers. Thank you so much for believing in my innocence and coming to my aid.

I would also like to beg your forgiveness for my effrontery in suggesting that perhaps you were an answer to my prayers in other areas as well. Never did I suspect that my propositions of correspondence would insult you so severely. Had I understood the level of your delicate and sensitive nature, I would have never broached such a subject.

In order to relieve you of further pains, I have decided to test my fortune and God's providence and set out for home this morning. I borrowed one of your yellow bonnets as well as your frilly house robe—the one lying at the foot of your bed. I am disguising myself as a woman in hopes that I will be able to arrive safely at the Louisiana border by midnight. You will also notice your other horse missing as well. Please understand that, as soon as I arrive safely home, I will forward sufficient money to cover the cost of your clothing and horse, as well as enough to reimburse you for my upkeep these last few days.

Please pray for me, Miss Isaacs, that I will

arrive safely to my home.

Admirably yours,
Rev. Noah Thorndyke

Her emotions tilting beyond all realms of logic, Angela covered her face with quivering hands and produced several trembling gasps. *Oh no! What have I done?* she thought, reliving the stony silence to which she had exposed Noah. Lambasting herself, Angela took complete blame for driving Noah to risk his life by leaving during the day, rather than waiting until nightfall. "If he gets killed, I will never forgive myself," she rasped against a shower of tears, drenching her cheeks.

But an image, completely detached from the moment, swam before her mind's eye—an image of an ebony stallion that greeted the dappled gray mare. *But I thought Mr. Thorndyke said he took the stallion!* Her mind racing in panic, Angela grabbed the note and reread the second paragraph to confirm that her memory was not deceiving her. Indeed, she had remembered correctly.

Next, Angela gazed dumbfounded at the crumpled yellow bonnet lying nearby. Her eyes widened. She held her breath. And the room seemed to spin around her. For the back of that bonnet was smudged with something Angela had failed to notice before now, something red, something that suspiciously resembled a blotch of blood. She grabbed the bonnet and inspected it more closely, to have her contemplations confirmed. *There is blood on the bonnet!*

Her pulse pounding in her temples, Angela abruptly stood, knocking over the ladder-backed chair and causing Grey to race across the kitchen, her tail straight up. In desperation, she stumbled out the kitchen door, across the yard, and back to the barn. She threw the door open and searched for the horse's saddle, where she always left it—hanging over the side of the stall. But it was gone. Puzzled, she glanced across the rest of the barn, to see the saddle, lying askew against the front wall. As if to confirm her worst fears, Angela stepped outside the barn and saw an image in the dust that left her mouth dry—drag marks, as if someone had pulled a lifeless body outside the barn. The dust also bore numerous boot prints, and Angela followed them with her eyes until they were lost amidst the grass.

"They found him," she whispered in disbelief, shaking her head. *But was it the law or the one who framed him?* Angela, not certain of the answer to that question, knew she had precious little time to spare. Regardless of the identity of Noah's captors, she needed to consult with Travis. She had no choice. This whole ordeal was bigger than anything Angela could possibly handle.

&

Noah jolted to consciousness when his backside met what felt like a hardwood floor. However, the dark hood over his pounding head blocked out any view of his surroundings. The sudden jar left his head thudding all the more. Spears of pain shot from his bound wrists and up his arms.

"You can take the hood off now, Mark," a masculine

voice snarled. "What Denham sees from here on ain't gonna make no difference."

Someone untied the strings of the black cotton sack and pulled it away.

Noah, thankful for the cool air that rushed upon his head, breathed deeply and glanced around the dingy, cluttered cabin that smelled of stale coffee. "I'm not Rupert Denham," Noah insisted, his tongue thick. He swiveled from his spot on the floor to face a man with brown eyes, stringy, dark hair, and a bushy beard to match.

" 'Course you ain't," the man sneered. "That would be me, now, wouldn't it? Surprise!" he mocked. "You just got yourself a twin brother."

At once, images of that troubling dream raced upon Noah. The mirror boy had made faces at Noah, as if to accuse him of some wrongdoing.

Noah took in the sharp angles of Denham's cheeks, the long, straight nose, the close-set eyes with heavy brows. Even though the hairy person before him looked more like a bear than a human being, Noah could detect the features that were very much his own.

For a flickering moment, the two sets of mirrored eyes held each other in soul-searching scrutiny. In that brief second of reunion with his twin, Noah caught a waver, a softening, in the evil-hearted Rupert.

"I—I speculated about having a twin, but I wasn't completely—completely sure," Noah said, his mind numb with amazement. He continued to search his brother's eyes, clinging to the hope that he could employ this uncanny sense of bonding and talk Rupert out of his devilish schemes.

However, with two quick blinks and a shake of his head, a fresh glaze of hate blazed from his soul and Denham snarled, "Well, you got more than a twin. You also got yerself a half-brother, too." Denham jerked his head toward the one he called Mark.

The young man observed Noah with a spark of speculation. "After your ma died, your paw married my ma. They soon had me. My ma died when I wasn't but eight."

"Paw died last year," Rupert said with a scheming edge to his voice. "Told me all about you 'fore he took his last breath. Told me you was so sick he feared you was gonna die, so he left you on the porch of a parson named Thorndyke." Rupert walked toward the rock fireplace and threw a couple of logs on the glowing embers.

"S–so you just—just decided to—to find me and—and let me hang instead of you. Is that it?" A warm trickle of blood oozed down the back of Noah's hand, and he winced with the pain of the ropes on his wrist.

"Yer a right smart one," Denham said, placing his booted foot in one of the rickety, gray dining chairs that squeaked its protest. "Smart enough to break jail once, and I don't 'magine I'm gonna let you have the chance agin."

"What's that supposed to mean?" Noah asked, his voice cracking.

"Soon as night falls and I can work under the cover of darkness, I'm fillin' you full of bullets and special deliverin' you to Sheriff Garner." His malicious smile revealed crooked, yellowed teeth.

Noah stared up at his brother, astounded that one who shared his looks could carry within him such a heart of darkness. Then, Noah recalled his own years on the river, years of gambling, years of stealing, years of rebellion against God. Looking back, Noah knew that corrupt lifestyle had nearly sucked him in completely. Only by the grace of God was he a righteous man today.

"Get busy makin' some coffee," Rupert growled in Mark's direction. The younger man, who shared Noah's coloring and heavy brows, glowered at Rupert. And Noah felt an undercurrent of bitterness flash between the two. However, Rupert ignored the younger man and focused his attention on the whiskey bottle he pulled from beneath the cot.

"Mark, would you please get me a drink of water," Noah said, trying to sound as polite as possible. Already, Noah was trying to form a means of escape. Getting Mark on his side might prove the only method.

ஐ

"Angela!" Rachel exclaimed. As she opened the door to the ranch house, it brushed against her full skirt, the color of rich coffee.

"Hello," Angela said forlornly. "Might I have a few minutes of your and Travis's time?"

"Of—of course," Rachel said, stepping aside to allow Angela to enter. "We just finished our noon meal. Have you eaten?"

"No."

"Is everything all right?" Rachel rushed. "You look terribly pale, and—"

"Everything is far from all right." Angela gathered up the skirt of her deep green church frock and stepped into the homey ranch house. Resolutely, she forced her emotions under control. The smells of beans, cornbread, and peach cobbler did little to ease the nausea churning in her midsection.

"Travis is in the parlor with Little Trav," Rachel said, flipping her waste-length, auburn braid over her shoulder. A toddler's delightful squeal erupted from the direction of the parlor, and Rachel led Angela the few paces into the room. Travis, on the floor with his son, looked up and produced a tired smile.

"Angela! What brings you here?" he asked. Respectfully standing to acknowledge the presence of a lady, he fumbled with the tail of his shirt, trying to discreetly tuck it back into his trousers.

Angela, gripping her reticule between stiff fingers gazed around the room—to the horsehair sofa, the worn rocking chair, the massive rock fireplace—she wanted to look anywhere but in the eyes of her relatives. At last, Angela screwed up the courage to state her mission. "I have some rather alarming news for both of you," she said in her school mistress voice then looked directly into Rachel's apprehensive eyes.

"Since Friday, I have been—I have—" Angela cleared her throat. "I—um—" Her mind raced with the possibility that the two of them would not believe that Noah was innocent, that perhaps they would think she had been a fool. But Angela knew different. Noah Thorndyke was not a murderer, and Angela had been far from a fool. She had to take the chance of Travis and Rachel thinking she was daft. "Friday morning, in my garden I discovered the man for whom the sheriff and constable have been searching. I have been hiding him in my storm cellar for the last two days," she blurted.

"What?" Travis burst forth, his eyes wide with astonishment.

"Oh, dear Lord, help us," Rachel whispered, lowering herself to the sofa, as if she no longer had the power to stand.

"Angela, that's considered aiding and abetting a criminal," Travis said. "You could face serious charges! And what about your safety? He hasn't tried to harm you, has he?"

"If the two of you will just listen to me," Angela said, sounding far more composed than her sweaty palms depicted. "The man I am—have been housing is not the criminal. His name is Noah Thorndyke. He has been terribly mistaken for Rupert Denham and, out of sheer desperation, he escaped the night before they were going to hang him. He is really a minister from Mansfield, Louisiana."

"Do you have solid proof of all this?" Travis asked.

Angela looked down at Little Trav, who toddled from his place in the middle of the rug toward his mother. "Yes," Angela said anxiously. "I have his word and I have the guidance of the Lord that he speaks the truth."

She imploringly gazed at Travis who dubiously observed her.

"That won't hold up in any court of law," he said, shaking his head as if he could hardly believe his ears. "And Angela," he continued gently, "you need to understand that most criminals will swear they're innocent." Travis, turning from her, scrubbed his fingers through his tawny hair as if he wanted to pull it out by the roots.

"You don't believe me!" Angela cried, her insides feeling as if they were full of cold bricks.

"Angela. . . ," Rachel said uncertainly.

"That man supposedly shot and killed a banker in Rusk," Travis said, spinning to face her. "It's a wonder he hasn't slit your throat."

"Will the two of you listen to me?" Angela demanded, stomping her foot. "The point of this whole trip is that he's gone! Someone came and dragged him off and his life might very well be in danger. I've got to have help!" she choked out, covering her face with her trembling gloved hands.

The sound of Rachel's skirts swishing against the wooden floors attested to her nearing. Soon, Angela felt a consoling arm around her shoulders and the reassurance gave her the strength to continue.

"I don't know if the law has come and gotten him or if it's Rupert Denham," she said blotting at the tears on her cheeks. "Mr. Thorndyke and I speculated that perhaps this Denham had framed him. They're exact look-alikes and Mr. Thorndyke even suspects that they might be twins. His father abandoned him when he was only three and he was adopted by a parson and his wife in Mansfield, Louisiana."

Travis neared and stopped within inches of Angela. At the same time, Little Trav produced an irritable cry, and Rachel bent to pick him up. Angela dared look into Travis's eyes, churning with enough misgivings to fill the sky with storm clouds. "Angela, I'm sorry," he said. "But this whole story sounds too fantastical for belief."

"Well, if it's any consolation," she snapped, vexed beyond the determined self-control she normally exhibited, "it's *your* sermon that helped me come to terms with part of what has happened this weekend." She pointed her index finger at his nose.

Blinking in astonishment, Travis held her gaze.

"*You're* the one who waxed eloquently this morning about letting the Lord guide you and trusting Him to help us, even with life's most difficult moments," she said, mimicking his voice's inflections. "Now, have you or have you not prayed about the snap decision you just made?" Angela asked, resorting to the same stern look to which she had exposed the sheriff two days before. The expression produced the exact same effect on Travis as it had the sheriff.

"Well. . . ," he said sheepishly.

"I think she has a point, Travis," Rachel said softly.

"Exactly what did you want me to do?" Travis asked slowly.

"I was thinking that perhaps you might agree to go into town and ask the constable if there had been any word about Noah—I mean, Mr. Thorndyke's capture. It would be natural for you to go, and I don't want him suspicious about why I'd ride into town and ask. I just talked with him yesterday and he told me then to call off school until Wednesday or until he told me otherwise. I just don't want to do anything to make him suspect. . . ." She left the rest unsaid.

"I'm sure the sheriff would wire the constable the minute Noah is caught," Angela said. "If he hasn't been captured by the law, then we can only assume that someone else has gotten him."

"How do you know he didn't just ride off?" Travis asked, his voice still indecisive.

"He—he *did* leave me a note to that effect," Angela said. "He told me in the note that he was taking my yellow bonnet and house robe, so that he would be disguised as a woman. He also said he'd be taking my ebony stallion and that he would send me money to cover the cost of everything he took. But the horse is still in the pasture. The bonnet, I found in my barn, with—with blood on it. And there are marks in the sand that look as if someone has been dragged through the dust."

Travis exchanged an increasingly urgent glance with Rachel. "I'll ride into Dogwood and see if the constable has word. Then, I'll swing by your place on my way home and give you a report," he said.

Rachel nodded, and Angela released a pent-up breath.

eleven

Noah's body ached all over. He had been sitting propped against the wall for the better part of an hour while Rupert took several swallows of whiskey then fell into a light sleep. The ropes binding Noah's wrists felt as if they were cutting tiny furrows into his flesh. Occasionally another trickle of blood oozed from the lacerations and the stinging increased all the more. The wound in his side produced an infrequent jabbing pain that only added to his discomfort.

Noah prayed until his mind was numb. He repeatedly quoted the Twenty-third Psalm to himself. And he thought of Miss Isaacs, his own guardian angel, who had taken a risk on believing his word. Furthermore, Noah decided that if he survived this ordeal, he would frequently write to Miss Isaacs, only stopping if she forbade him to continue with the most severe and continual reprimands. The longer Noah thought about her, the more he believed that she might very well be an answer to his prayers. Only time would tell, but Noah would not take just one "no" as an answer from her. *You will have to tell me "no" at least six times before I will stop writing you, Miss Isaacs*, he thought with resolution.

Mark entered from outside and tossed another log on the fire. He glanced at the sleeping Rupert and walked toward Noah. From a sheath strapped to his thigh, the younger man whipped out a knife with a long, gleaming blade. Noah's gut tightened in dread of Mark's next move.

The young man bent over Noah's feet and cut the cord binding his legs. "Get on your feet," Mark whispered. "We're going for a little ride."

Shocked, Noah began struggling to his feet. As often as possible in their brief acquaintance, Noah had smiled at Mark, been polite, and tried to show the young man the respect Rupert was far from exhibiting. Noah's soul filled with a rush of hope. Perhaps his plan was working and Mark had decided to help his half-brother escape.

However, the first step in that process included Noah's standing—a step that proved more difficult than he ever imagined. He was stiff from the cramped position, and the wound in his side produced intermittent stabs of pain. Silently, he pleaded with his muscles to provide enough strength to rise. At last, Mark reached down and grabbed his arm, supplying Noah with the appropriate support he needed to gain his footing.

"Head for the horses outside," Mark said under his breath.

Noah didn't waste a moment arguing with him. As quietly as possible, he walked to the door, only pausing long enough for Mark to open it for him. Noah glanced over his shoulder to see Rupert stirring in his sleep, and he hastened out the door. Silently, Mark shut the door and, without a word, cut the ropes binding Noah's raw wrists. Immediately, Noah pulled his aching arms in front of him and gingerly touched his chaffed wrists.

"I'm going to get on the bay. Get on behind me after I mount," Mark whispered from behind.

Noah looked toward two horses—one a bay, the other a palomino—both tethered to one of the numerous trees. His mind racing with anticipation, Noah nodded his ready agreement. In seconds, Mark assisted him atop the bay gelding and he hung onto the saddle's back rim as the horse trotted up the worn trail, winding through the woods. The sun, inching its way toward the western horizon, suggested the hour was between three and four. Noah wondered whether Miss Isaacs had spent the afternoon regretting his departure or reveling in relief that he now was gone.

"Where are we going?" Noah whispered, his head still pounding with every word he spoke.

"Wherever you want to go," Mark said, glancing over his shoulder. "We're only about twenty minutes from where we got you. Do you want to return there?"

Noah thought of Miss Isaacs, of her probable discovery that he had not taken the ebony stallion after all. He wondered if she suspected that he had been kidnapped during his attempts to leave. Noah would like to speak to her one last time before trying to make it to Louisiana. Perhaps the smartest thing would be to ask her permission to stay in her cellar until nightfall. For, after the recent turn in circumstances, Noah did not feel physically capable of striking out on his own. Miss Isaacs had once mentioned driving him part of the way, and Noah wondered if her offer still stood.

"Yes, let's go back to where I was," Noah said, pausing before posing his next question. "Why are you doing this?"

"Because you're innocent and don't deserve to die, and I've put up with Rupert all I'm goin' to. I'm cuttin' out on him. I never did take to all his stealin' and connivin'. I'm tired of being on the edge of it all. Our paw might not 'a' been perfect, but he shore didn't raise us to be robbers and murderers."

"I know Rupert is wanted for murder. Are you?" Noah asked, hoping for a negative answer.

"Nope," Mark said. "I ain't never killed a person in my whole life. Don't ever plan to either. And as far as the stealin'. . .I only done what I was forced to do."

A sudden rush of camaraderie blanketed Noah and his half-brother. There was something very decent in the sound of Mark Denham's voice. Even though this man in front of him had assisted in his capture, he *was* Noah's brother and he *was* aiding in his escape. "Tell me more about our father," Noah said.

However, Mark's reply was cut off by the explosion of a bullet and Rupert's raucous cursing, echoing through the woods.

"Hang on!" Mark commanded before burying his spurs into the horse's flanks. The animal bolted forward, and Noah's side protested against the sudden lurch. Another gunshot rang out and a bullet whizzed past Noah's head. He joined Mark's instinctive duck as even more bullets pelted the trees. And Noah relived another such ride only two days before—a ride that left him lying in Miss Isaac's garden, a wounded and desperate man.

❧

Angela, exhausted from fatigue, lay on her velvet sofa and watched the fireplace's glowing embers. Anxiously, she waited for word from Travis. Angela looked at the watch hanging on the chain around her neck and noted that three-thirty was swiftly approaching. Travis should arrive any moment with a report from Constable Parker. Once again, Angela rose from the couch to pace her living room. With each pace, she relived her harsh treatment of Mr. Thorndyke and cringed with the recall of every word. *How could I have been so callused?* She could only pray that Noah would not die before she had the chance to beg his forgiveness. Angela, tightly gripping her hands, beseeched the Lord to protect him, wherever he might be.

A muffled shot rang out, and Angela jumped. She raced to her parlor window to see no signs of an intruder. Yet, an even closer shot attested to the presence of a nearing gunman. Angela, her heart wildly palpitating, ran to look out the window in the kitchen. From this vantage point, she could see a horse galloping toward her house at breakneck speed. Upon its back sat two men. One of them appeared to be Noah. "Jump!" the man in front hollered, and Noah lunged from the horse as it sped away from the house. Angela, gasping for air, watched as Noah hit the ground to roll several feet and stop near her back steps. Another shot rang from the woods before a second horseman gal-loped from the forest and into the clearing. Flinging open the back door, Angela grabbed Noah's arm and assisted him as he struggled up the steps, to collapse into her kitchen. She slammed the door and slumped against it. But when a bullet pierced the wood just above her head, Angela hit the floor beside Noah.

"It's Rupert Denham," Noah gasped, his face contort-ing in pain. "Mark—Mark and I were h–hoping he wouldn't see me jump, and—and would continue to chase Mark."

"Looks like that plan didn't work," Angela said grimly.

"Rupert *is* my t–twin, and he wants me d–dead!" Gripping his right arm, Noah groaned.

"You've been shot again!" Angela cried, noticing the sickening blotch of blood oozing from beneath his hand.

"Lock the door!" Noah commanded, scooting him-self farther into the kitchen.

Angela scrambled to secure the wooden bar firmly in place only seconds before the sound of pounding horse's hooves stopped outside the door. "I'm going after my shotgun," Angela said, racing toward her bedroom. She grabbed a handful of bullets from the top drawer of her chest of drawers then reached for the shotgun standing beside her bed. Her father had insisted upon Angela's expertise with a firearm when she moved to the cottage. And every month, the aging gentleman paid a special visit to his daughter for the sole purposes of shooting. As

Angela gripped the gun and watched the door's wooden bar bulge against the strain of the man slamming his body into it, she prepared to pull the trigger and thanked her Lord that her father had never missed one of their marksman appointments.

As she suspected, the door at last crashed inward, and a tall man with a wiry beard and eyes like a demon stumbled into her kitchen. Angela gave him no time to gain his balance. She pointed the gun at his legs and pulled the trigger. He howled in pain and lunged forward, falling at her feet as if he were a felled tree. His revolver flew from his hand and spun across the kitchen floor. Angela automatically inserted another bullet into the gun's chamber, snapped it shut, and braced it against her shoulder.

"If you try anything stupid, I'll be forced to shoot you again," she said precisely, yet her legs trembled so violently she feared she would collapse.

The smell of gunpowder permeated the kitchen, and the man on the floor writhed in pain. Angela suspected he would be incapacitated for quite some while.

"You—you saved my life a–again," Noah gasped, pulling himself to a sitting position. "How can—can I ever repay you?"

Travis's firm knock resounded through the cottage. "Angela! Angela!" he yelled, then rattled the front door. "Are you in there? Angela? I heard gunshots!"

"Come—come to the kitchen door," Angela hollered.

In seconds, Travis rushed into the kitchen. "I heard shots, and—" He stopped short when he saw Rupert

Denham lying on the floor, with Noah a few feet away.

Angela, never taking the gun off Denham, bit her lips and choked on a sob of relief. "I—I can't believe I've done it, but some–somehow, I managed to cap–capture the criminal," she said.

His eyes round, Travis stared from Denham to Angela to Noah. He pushed back his felt hat, shook his head, and whistled in disbelief.

❧

By noon the next day, all of Dogwood buzzed with the news of Angela Isaacs' heroic capture of the notorious killer. The stories flew high and wide and were so variant in their details that Angela felt certain no one suspected she had housed Noah Thorndyke for two days. Presently, with the exception of Dr. Engle, the whole town seemed to think that the first she had ever seen of Noah was when he crawled into her kitchen seconds before Denham made his entry.

When Angela arrived at Dr. Engle's office to pay Noah a visit, the doctor exposed her to a welcoming smile. "It's a good thing you're here," he said, removing his spectacles to rub his bushy, gray brows. "Mr. Thorndyke has been restless to see ya all morning." The doctor eyed her speculatively, and Angela returned his gaze with as bland an expression as she could muster.

According to Travis, when he delivered Noah to Dr. Engle's office for treatment of the gunshot wounds, the insightful doctor demanded to know who had tended the first injury. Travis swore the doctor to secrecy before telling the whole story of Angela's hiding and nursing Noah.

"Humph," Dr. Engle said. "To look at you, you'd think you didn't give one flip whether the man lives or dies, but I think I know different," he continued with an audacious wink.

"Has he had a good morning?" Angela asked, purposefully maintaining her composure.

"Yes, quite good. Fortunately, the bullet wasn't lodged too deep and didn't chip a bone. Looks like the Lord was lookin' out for that man on all sides. The whole town is talkin' about the way he escaped jail, and word has it Sheriff Garner is supposed to appear some time today to present a formal apology."

"He should," Angela said with gravity.

A bell's impatient ring sounded from the patient's room. "Well, go on in," the doctor said, jerking his head toward the room. "He's waitin' on you and is about to drive me to distraction with that bell." The doctor walked toward his kitchen, all the while mumbling, "I'll be, if there ain't another romance brewin' in that room. Seems like every time a man gets himself injured in these parts he winds up in that bed and next thing you know—boom—he's hitched."

Angela, smiling slightly, remembered when Dr. Engle's nurse, Magnolia Alexander, wound up marrying one of her own patients, who also happened to be Travis Campbell's brother. Yesterday at church, Magnolia and Levi had seemed more like newlyweds than a couple married two years who now had a baby.

Because of Magnolia's marriage to Levi, the doctor lost a nurse to matrimony, but wound up gaining a wife himself, Sarah Douglas, who now served as his part-time nurse.

Dismissing these thoughts, Angela walked across the rustic outer office that smelled of kerosene and antiseptic. She paused outside the room's door long enough to straighten her hat and rub her damp palms across her full, indigo skirt. With as much dignity as she could muster, Angela opened the door and stepped into the room. Noah's slow smile of pleasure left her heart beating far past the comfort zone.

"I've been waiting on you all morning," he said, reaching for her hand.

Without hesitation, Angela stepped to his side and placed her hand in his. Her face warmed, and she chose to focus on the starched white sheets that swathed the patient. Through the closed window, the muffled sounds of Dogwood's busy streets punctuated the awkward moment. When Noah's hand tightened on Angela's she shyly pulled it away and turned to walk the brief distance to the wooden rocking chair. Head bent, she sat in the chair then immediately stood back up. Fidgeting, Angela walked the few inches toward the window and stared at the numerous buggies, wagons, and pedestrians, rushing here and there.

"There's something—" she began, turning to face Noah.

"Miss Isaacs," he said simultaneously.

She produced a smile of chagrin. "Excuse me."

"No, please excuse me," Noah said with a chivalrous nod of his head.

"I was just going to tell you that—that—" Angela nervously licked her lips. "That I feel I must apologize for my dreadful behavior toward you during your hour of dire need. I treated you in a most abhorrent fashion, and for that, I am deeply ashamed and—and hope that you can find it in your heart to extend your forgiveness."

"Would you care to expound upon what I should forgive you for?" Noah quirked one brow, and his dark eyes danced with merriment. "All I remember is a gracious lady who not only rescued me from a posse bent on hanging me, but also bore arms against an outlaw trying to take my life."

Angela, her heart pounding all the more furiously, debated exactly what to say. "Well, I. . .I. . .you requested my permission to—to—" She cleared her throat and gripped her reticule until she was certain it might scream. "To correspond with me, and I—"

"Ah, the correspondence," he said, breaking into an endearing smile. "Of course. Thank you so much for broaching that important subject." His smile increased, and Angela had the uncanny feeling that she had just stepped through a door he held wide open. "It might come as quite a surprise to you, Miss Isaacs, that, as far as I am concerned, the issue of our corresponding has long been settled."

Her heart sinking, Angela assumed that he must have taken her initial negative answer as the final one. Inside, she floundered for an appropriate way to hint that she had reconsidered his offer without seeming brazen. Yet another troubling thought struck her. *What if he has decided he would rather not correspond?* She turned back to the window, pledging to take every possible means to ensure that Mr. Thorndyke did not detect her disappointment.

"Would it terribly upset you to learn that I decided during my brief season of captivity that I would indeed write to you, whether you initially agreed or not?"

Angela, her eyes wide, spun to face him. Her Sunday-best skirt swirled around her ankles, producing a whisper that reflected the delighted gasp escaping her lips.

Noah observed her with the expression of a smitten school boy, his eyes pools of admiration, his lips tilted in an uncertain twist. His hand stirred atop the light quilt covering him, suggesting that his emotions were as taut as her own. "You see, I came to the conclusion that a woman of your character was worth pursuing and that, in order for me to not correspond, you would have to deliver unto me a series of severe and continual reprimands."

"Mr. Thorndyke, I don't know what to say," Angela rushed primly, her disconcerted mind reeling with the implications of his admission.

"Well, if you were to say that you would be agreeable to my writing to you, as far as I'm concerned, that would be a highly appropriate reply." Noah shifted in the bed as if he were anxious for her affirmation of his suggestion.

Angela, her palms damp, diminished the distance

between them and Noah once more reached for her hand. This time, she didn't pull away when his fingers enclosed hers. Without blinking, Noah held her gaze and tugged her gloved hand toward his lips. Gently, he pressed his lips against the back of her hand and held them there while he implored her with his eyes to eventually give him a chance at more than just correspondence.

Like an avalanche, the melting ice around her heart cracked, and a flood of warmth filled her being. Angela, her eyes stinging, rapidly blinked and experienced an unexpected surge of panic as Mr. Thorndyke removed his lips. The last time she felt like this, the recipient of her admiration scorned her.

"You might find it interesting to learn that Mr. Travis Campbell has already been by this morning," Noah said with pleasure. "It seems that he is heading up a pulpit committee, and he asked my permission to place my name as a possible candidate."

Angela's alarm increased as her mind projected the possibilities of the next few months: Noah, moving in just up the road from her; their initial correspondence turning to a full-blown courtship; the minister's subsequent proposal; Angela's being forced to make a decision.

"I'm—I'm not c–certain I'm—I'm ready for—for—" Angela cleared her throat and resorted to the outward composure that years of teaching had bequeathed her. "I will agree to our corresponding, Mr. Thorndyke, but I must be honest and tell you that I am not certain I am ready for any kind of long-term romantic attachment," she rushed, gently tugging her hand from his grasp. "If you move here, I hope it is for the sole reason that you feel the Lord's direction, otherwise—"

"Who was he, Miss Isaacs? Who was the one responsible for the painful shadows in your eyes?"

"I'm afraid we haven't known each other long enough to discuss such—"

"The circumstances of our acquaintance have long since circumvented the norms of propriety. Already, you know my life's story. All I ask is that you share your painful experience so that I might better understand you and therefore take the proper precautions in developing our acquaintance."

With a sigh, Angela peered deeply into Noah's eyes and relived the moment she had met him only three days ago. He had invaded her life in the most outlandish state of affairs and instigated Angela's doing what she had vowed to never do again—foolishly trust the word of a man. But somehow, Noah Thorndyke had seemed an exemplary man of reputable honor, even in the face of being an escaped "criminal." Now, despite knowing him only days, Angela decided to share her broken heart.

With as brief an explanation as possible, she detailed the occurrences that led to her intense mortification and left her the subject of sympathetic gossip for months. "I have had a problem with trust since that day," she honestly stated. "And I am only just now coming to the point of considering. . .that is to say that—that my agreeing to correspond with you is nothing short of a miracle within itself. However, I still need time to—"

"Yes, of course you do. I heartily agree. And I must assure you that I, in no way, intend to push you into any agreement that would leave you less than comfortable."

Angela reflected on the fact that she had been anything but comfortable since the minute she found Noah Thorndyke in her garden. "Furthermore," she continued, desperate to be completely honest with him. "You seem to insist upon the impression that I am some sort of spiritual woman of virtue of sorts that—"

"Oh, but you are," he insisted. "There are precious few women who would have—"

"No, I'm not," Angela firmly replied. "I feel it highly necessary to emphasize, that I have attended church for these past years only as a fulfillment of the terms of my teaching contract. And as I have already told you, it was only the dire straits in which you arrived at my home that drove me back to prayer."

"Well, as long as the end result is gained, that is all that matters. Nonetheless, Angela. . ." He paused and exposed her to a pleading gaze. "May I address you by your first name?"

She hesitated but a second. "Yes, of course," Angela said, her cheeks warming again.

"And please, don't hesitate to call me Noah," he replied. With a daring gleam in his eye, he reached, once more, for her hand.

Angela bit her lips as she observed the long, slender fingers that covered her hand. "Of course."

"As I was saying, I think that perhaps the Lord

dropped me into your life for a variety of reasons—many of which we have yet to realize." He waited but a poignant second before continuing. "And I'm thrilled to hear of your renewed interest in the things of God. Assuredly, you are a woman whose heart He can touch. Otherwise, you wouldn't have been open to His guidance concerning my plight."

"There was a time or two I almost turned you in," she said, candidly watching him for any negative response.

"Yes, I know," he replied without a blink. "I would most likely have wavered just as you did. That is understandable, but in the end, you did the right thing."

"I guess that's all the Lord asks of us, isn't it?" Angela said, reflecting upon the grace that God had extended to her. Grace that had cleansed her disobedience. Grace that was undeserved, yet fully embraced.

epilogue

Eight months later, Angela sat on the second pew of the Dogwood Community Church as her husband of three months took his spot behind the pulpit. Before announcing his text, Noah turned a beaming smile upon her, a smile that spoke of his happiness and even a secretive nuance of pride. For it was that very morning that Angela had shared her suspicions with her husband. She discreetly touched the waistline of her navy blue suit and wondered how much longer she would be able to wear the snug-fitting skirt. Soon, she would discreetly announce the news to the school board and alert them that they would need to find a replacement.

Beside her, Mark Denham leaned sideways, fumbling with his large Bible. "What verse did he say?" the former ruffian asked.

"I have no idea," Angela blissfully whispered, smiling at her new brother-in-law. After the trial and hanging of Rupert Denham, Noah had stepped forward to defend his younger brother and had negotiated an acquittal for Mark. Part of the terms of his acquittal involved Noah's agreeing to Mark's living with him. Mark testified to the Lord's working in his life even before he met Noah. Soon after moving into the parsonage with Noah, Mark had readily accepted Christ as his Savior and was flourishing under the influence of his godly brother.

As the service continued, Angela gazed upon her handsome husband and reflected over the preceding months. She and Noah had corresponded only a few weeks when he accepted the call to pastor Dogwood Community Church. Bit by bit, the Lord had worked a miracle of healing within Angela and she soon gave her whole heart to Noah. Sighing, she smiled with contentment and tried to concentrate upon the words of the man behind the pulpit. But Angela was too enamored with the man himself to contemplate his words.

At last, Noah called for the benediction, then the people visited and disbursed, until only Angela and Noah remained near the back door. Noah, preparing to open the door, paused and turned to his bride. With a soft smile, he reached for Angela and she gladly leaned into his embrace. Reveling in the pleasurable warmth that spread through her, Angela wrapped her arms around him and soaked in the ardor of his affection.

"I never dreamed that night when I was waiting to be hanged that God was in the middle of working a miracle," Noah said with wonder.

Angela pulled away far enough to gently stroke Noah's face, smooth from his morning shave. "And I never dreamed that I was hiding my future husband in my cellar or that. . ." She paused as an unexplainable joy welled up within her soul and manifested itself with the warm tears pooling in her eyes. Silently, Angela touched her midsection and Noah covered her hand with his.

"That I would be blessed with two angels," he finished for her.

A Letter To Our Readers

Dear Reader:

In order that we might better contribute to your reading enjoyment, we would appreciate your taking a few minutes to respond to the following questions. We welcome your comments and read each form and letter we receive. When completed, please return to the following:

Rebecca Germany, Fiction Editor
Heartsong Presents
PO Box 719
Uhrichsville, Ohio 44683

1. Did you enjoy reading *Texas Angel?*
   ☐ Very much. I would like to see more books
      by this author!
   ☐ Moderately
      I would have enjoyed it more if _____
      _____
      _____

2. Are you a member of **Heartsong Presents**? Yes ☐ No ☐
   If no, where did you purchase this book?_____
   _____

3. How would you rate, on a scale from 1 (poor) to 5 (superior),
   the cover design?_____

4. On a scale from 1 (poor) to 10 (superior), please rate the
   following elements.

   _____ Heroine   _____ Plot

   _____ Hero   _____ Inspirational theme

   _____ Setting   _____ Secondary characters

5. These characters were special because_____

_____

_____

6. How has this book inspired your life?_____

_____

_____

7. What settings would you like to see covered in future
   Heartsong Presents books?_____

_____

_____

8. What are some inspirational themes you would like to see
   treated in future books?_____

_____

_____

9. Would you be interested in reading other **Heartsong
   Presents** titles?   Yes ❑   No ❑

10. Please check your age range:
    ❑ Under 18   ❑ 18-24   ❑ 25-34
    ❑ 35-45   ❑ 46-55   ❑ Over 55

11. How many hours per week do you read?_____

Name _____

Occupation _____

Address _____

City _____ State _____ Zip _____

Prairie BRIDES

Set on the open plains when saying "I do" often meant a commitment to a life of hard work. But, love has the ability to shine over any circumstance and light the bride's eyes with sparkles of hope. Four all new stories by authors JoAnn A. Grote, Linda Ford, Linda Goodnight, and Amy Rognlie.

paperback, 352 pages, 5 ⁹⁄₁₆" x 8"

❤ ❤ ❤ ❤ ❤ ❤ ❤ ❤ ❤ ❤ ❤ ❤ ❤ ❤ ❤ ❤ ❤ ❤

❤ ❤ ❤ ❤ ❤ ❤ ❤ ❤ ❤ ❤ ❤ ❤ ❤ ❤ ❤ ❤ ❤ ❤

Hearts♥ng Presents
Love Stories Are Rated G!

That's for godly, gratifying, and of course, great! If you love a thrilling love story, but don't appreciate the sordidness of some popular paperback romances, **Heartsong Presents** is for you. In fact, **Heartsong Presents** is the *only inspirational romance book club* featuring love stories where Christian faith is the primary ingredient in a marriage relationship.

Sign up today to receive your first set of four, never before published Christian romances. Send no money now; you will receive a bill with the first shipment. You may cancel at any time without obligation, and if you aren't completely satisfied with any selection, you may return the books for an immediate refund.

Imagine. . .four new romances every four weeks—two historical, two contemporary—with men and women like you who long to meet the one God has chosen as the love of their lives. . . all for the low price of $9.97 postpaid.

To join, simply complete the coupon below and mail to the address provided. **Heartsong Presents** romances are rated G for another reason: They'll arrive *Godspeed!*